The Girl Beneath the Lion

André Pieyre de Mandiargues

The Girl Beneath the Lion

TRANSLATED BY RICHARD HOWARD

GROVE PRESS INC.   NEW YORK

*Grove Press Books and Evergreen Books
are published by Barney Rosset at Grove Press Inc.*
795 Broadway   New York 3, N. Y.

Type set by The Polyglot Press, New York
MANUFACTURED IN THE UNITED STATES OF AMERICA

The Girl Beneath the Lion is published in
four editions:

An Evergreen Book (E-126)

A cloth bound edition

A specially bound and signed edition
of 26 copies, numbered A through Z

A specially bound and signed edition
of 4 copies, *hors commerce,* numbered
1 through 4

To Bona

Sea Lilies

I could never forget the sight of these great white flowers, growing only a foot or two from the sea. They were the fantastic ornament of the beach at Orosei, in Sardinia, and I had never seen them before this encounter at the end of a scorching summer, on the deserted sands where we came every day.

Not very high, the mountain that forms almost the whole of the island's eastern coast fell sheer to the sea at either end of the beach, hollowing a bay between; the yellowish gray, almost naked rock still managed to produce a few myrtles, Barbary figs, and other prickly plants. In the center, running down a narrow valley, a stream disappeared into the sand, forming a marsh of brackish water rimmed with blackened roots, and reeds behind them. Often, when you walked this way, snakes would hurry into the water at your approach, with that arrow-like movement that makes them look even more wicked than on land. Every evening, toward sunset, a great flock of sheep (several thousand) tumbled down a zigzag path which, for centuries surely, their hard little hooves had worn into the hillside; there was a cloud of dust, and they shouldered each other into the reeds to drink from the marsh. The rest of the time we were quite alone. A cabin, its walls woven from the reeds, served as a shelter (against what?). The sea lilies, that flecked the beach with white, were thus the seal of our solitude.

I have since learned that they are called *pancratia*, from the Latin *pancratium maritimum*, and perhaps the shape of their seed, which—to a charitable eye—resembles a clenched fist, is responsible for a name that rather capriciously relates them to the ancient Greek pugilists. The more common name, sea lily, is also a prettier one. Actually, they are not lilies at all, but a variety of giant narcissus (they belong to the narcissus family) or amaryllis (only slightly smaller than the fragrant pink flower cultivated on the Riviera for bouquets and lovers' triumphs). Their perfume is a compromise between that of both flowers, fresh and at the same time heavy, strong, and intoxicating.

Beach plants, especially when they grow near enough the water to catch the spindrift carried by the wind from the sea, are generally brown, red, or bluish gray. Yet the sea lily's stems and lanceolate leaves proclaim a green so raw they remind you rather of spring meadows, or early forest growth. That such vegetation can appear, develop, flower, even fructify in the salt-impregnated sand is already something of a prodigy. But even more wonderful is the fact that an arable soil, far from being necessary to its sustenance, destroys the sea lily, and if you try to transplant it to your garden, to cultivate it by ordinary horticultural means, it soon rots and dies. Better still (or rather, a stranger and more surprising fact), when I had broken off a stalk with neither bulb nor roots attached, thrusting it into the dry reeds of the shelter wall, it remained for over a week as fresh as on the day I had picked it. It attracted a late-afternoon moth, the bindweed sphinx, which came to suck up nectar from its corollas, each time just before the rush of sheep at the water hole.

Such matters, though I have called them extraordinary, are doubtless quite common and will surprise no one with a botanical turn of mind. There is no need to go as far as Sardinia to see the sea lilies, which flourish also on the Ile du Levant, on the island of Porquerolles, and formerly on the beach at Giens when there were not so many tourists. But in my eyes, the marvel remains. It is in a kind of audacious, adventurous exile; it is in the unexpected presence of this (admirable) plant in regions which would reasonably appear hostile to it, or at least alien; it is in the rising of a sap so rich and which is nourished only by the poorest sand. The flower's beauty insolently proclaims itself, and insolent is the brilliance of its green foliage, gleaming richly against the arid sand. One is similarly moved (to joy or resentment, according to one's temperament) by any show of luxury in a country of desolation.

And then, the white cones of the sea lilies, when I had looked at them a long time where they grew against the dark sand, in the blinding light of noon, grew starred upon my retinas, constellations in their blank decor, as if they had been turned on, like lamps against the night sky. Their fragrance was at its paroxysmal peak, and charged the unmoving air with great gusts of perfume, as on summer nights when you walk near a bed of heliotrope, verbena, or red geraniums. Noon, doubtless because of the shadows either missing or minor, and because the heat has driven men to seek their houses (or the

houses to seek their men . . .), and because the
fields and beaches are abandoned, is intimate with
night. I do not mean, of course, the obvious relation
between the *hours* of noon and midnight; it is the
pancratia (certainly an inappropriate name, I shall
not use it again) of Orosei that have given me this
little *aperçu*, almost a revelation.

The Girl Beneath the Lion

The beach of Santa Lucia di Siniscola is a long sandbar between the Gulf of Sardinia and a brackish sound where the reeds flourish. Lining the inland shore is a series of low, pointed dunes littered with shells and overgrown with dry thistles; behind these are dunes still higher, backed by a row of young pines planted to sustain a soil so fugitive that every breath of wind displaces it. Some eucalyptus trees, also of recent growth, show above the pines stunted from being too closely set, the pistachios, the cane-apples, and the scrub myrtles that cover the island, where every plant or animal is dwarfed or crabbed in comparison with the mainland species.

Clumps of seaweed the storms have uprooted and cast ashore—black and green underwater, whitened where they are exposed—fringe the beach for several miles in varying abundance, like hair on the body of

3

a colossal girl, their odor strong but not unpleasant. Between the reeds, when the inland shore is accessible, lodge pieces of driftwood, roots of strangely human or bestial shape, every sort of rubbish and debris. A mind sensitive to the nature of things cannot help but establish a relation between the violent purity of the gulf, salt and abstergent, and the almost secret corruption of the sound, its semi-stagnant, isolated ponds covered with a leathery yellow froth that might be foam or merely another form of vegetable life.

Far beyond the village and the bathing beach, the sound communicates with the sea by a channel across the sandbar, a narrow trench in which the current reverses with the tide (here, as everywhere along the Mediterranean, of minor amplitude). The channel is regularly dredged, despite the loess the east wind clogs it with, so that fish—white mullet for the most part—can reach the ponds and feed richly enough to become fat and profitable for the fisheries. Here too the dark-green, thin-legged river crabs that live among the reeds scuttle back and forth at night (but most frequently when there is a moon). Eddies and tremors on the surface when the gnats fly low betoken a teeming life among the

water weeds. *Ichnusa*—abounding in fish—was the
ancient name for Sardinia.

Beyond the channel the beach continues, a series
of monotonous dunes in front of the young pines,
as far as La Caletta at the tip of its shining arc,
where the sand comes to an end. There are a few
houses among the gray trees, and a tiny harbor indicated by a square tower. The harbor is a depend-
ency at Siniscola, set at the mountains' feet and
once the barony's chief port, now only a disinherited
town at the sun's mercy, breeding clouds of flies
between columns of dust raised by the children
playing, the little donkeys trotting. Far behind the
tower, where a fire is kept burning after dark, the
sky frays out against the serrations of Coda di Ca-
vallo, a cape that looks as though it had just landed
on the water like a whip cracked by some gigantic
hand. Still farther off-shore—fallen, perhaps, from
the same hand that cast the cape out to sea—a series
of purple islets, a sugar-loaf reef and the larger
islands of Molara and Tavolara, intercept the horizon so suddenly they suggest a world inaccessible
except to fancy, where no matter how timidly the
dreamer yearning for paradise approaches them,
their beauty still promises the lost creatures of fable,
chimeras whose feathers and fur are variegated only

according to the laws of imagination, worthy in every detail of the mineral fantasy he has chosen for their habitat. The dreamer, of course, is deceived, yet the reality of these islands, aside from a few goats and occasionally, dozing in some grotto, a seal known as a "sea cow," offers a society of fishing birds so various that he might marvel at their multitudes for months together and not regret the glamors of his artificial paradise.

Behind Siniscola the arid rock of Mount Albo rises like the wall of a reverberatory furnace. The plain before it and the dusty town swelter in the hot winds reflected from its face, and the gardens must be watered often to sustain their citrons in the failing earth. The mountain culminates in a scaly yellow crest, a giant lizard's back against which the clouds tear themselves to pieces. But in summer the sky is almost always clear.

All nature is a sanctuary, from one point of view or another; that is—setting aside the concept of creation itself—all nature is inhabited by a god (or by several). Here at Siniscola, the god could be only Pan.

Vanina had been in his domain for three days.

Lying on the sand, the girl had covered her face with a corner of her beach robe, as it is said the

emperors did after the battle was lost and retreat
cut off, in order to yield themselves entirely to the
victor's discretion, expecting him to put them to
death or in irons. Breathing through a fold she had
arranged in the spongy material (for she was solici-
tous of such trifles as girls her age understand, who
like to provide for all the mere details of life), Vanina thought about the defeated emperor, spread
her legs apart to expose them better to the sun. She
also thought about the Oriental captivity of legend-
ary queens, and casting about for the source of such
images, decided it was the odor of the oil she had
generously smeared herself with to protect her skin
against the first days' sunburn, an odor her im-
provised cowl had concentrated as if her head were
inside a gas bubble. There was enough musk, honey,
and bitter almonds in its aroma to suggest the *souk*
or the sheepfold, and with a thread of perspiration
as well, the palms of her hands providing a cushion
for the nape of her neck, the harem was not far off.

When she opened her eyes, she saw blue and
white stripes an inch away from her lashes against
a glowing background that was the web of the
material itself. It was impossible to tell how long
the sun had been shining through it, for the first
effect of its fires was to benumb all sense of time.

She would cease being a slave now. With an effort (for it is difficult and seldom agreeable to regain one's liberty) she stretched out her hand, groped for the wrist watch rolled up inside her handkerchief, and drew it under the dazzling veil.

Almost noon. It was not surprising that the vertical rays had turned her beach robe into a grill; that despite her Chaldean oils—diluted now by sweat besides—she felt an ominous prickling down her thighs and along her shoulders. If she remained where she was, she would certainly risk pain tonight and peeling for several days afterward, perhaps even the disfiguring sores she had often seen on the skin of English or Norwegian girls. She sat up, letting the emperor's mantle slip from her, breathing deeply to restore her blood to its customary course. Revived, she touched the arm of the big girl lying next to her, spread out on her belly like a sun-drugged dog.

"Juliette," she said, "wake up! It's late. Let's go in the water."

The sleeping girl stretched, not too good-naturedly, before turning over. Of coarser build than Vanina, Juliette had shorter legs in proportion to her body, thicker arms, and a much less supple waist; her squat neck rose from a boy's chest, and her cropped hair showed sepia and yellow and rust like

a young birch in autumn, though with nothing of
its bark's first whiteness, for her skin burned or
freckled in the sun, never really bronzed. As she
padded down to the water on all fours, her eyes
fixed, neither squinting nor blinking, defying the
glare that would have blinded any other northern
girl, her pupils assumed so perfectly the very color
of the sea where it lay beneath them, that even the
fine gravel on the bottom seemed to lie within their
transparence.

Vanina had stuffed her hair into a rubber cap and
fastened the strap under her chin. She put her watch
and her dark glasses in an orange bag so bright that
even the sun could not subdue its flamboyance, and
it glowed at noon like a live coal in starlight. On top
of it she folded her beach robe, then Juliette's, with
a stone to cover them, more as a precaution against
some stray animal or marauding child than to keep
them from blowing away, for the air was quite still.
Then she rejoined her friend who was on her feet
now, waiting tall and resolute in the great empty
space her body loomed against with a kind of splendor.

"You're strong, Juliette," Vanina said. "I'm never
afraid as long as I hear you swimming behind me.
You'd save me." And she laughed, knowing she

could swim as far and as fast as the other girl.

The sand, which the sun had slowly braised while the girls were browning like meat in a pan, now left a painful cushion on their soles with every step. The lighter of the two, Vanina played at being a feather, trying to weigh as little as if she were making her way over a glowing stove or across the dome of a roaring furnace—situations rare enough for even dreams to have left her ill-prepared to meet them. Involuntarily, the result achieved was a precipitous tiptoe movement; it looked as if she were dancing.

In contrast with the burning sand, the sea felt icy when the water touched their feet, and they stopped before it reached above their knees, so brutally had the cold seized them, so quickly had it entered their bodies and insinuated its paralysis within their very hearts. But they made none of the extravagant gestures of girls bathing when they know they are being watched or when boys tease them; they did not splash and scream, nor jostle each other, pretending to fall or to be frightened, for Vanina had often derided in Juliette's hearing the silliness of such behavior, and Juliette, who with other companions would have thrown herself about as wildly as the next, now made every effort to remain calm and earn her friend's respect. One behind

the other, they walked deliberately forward on the
even sand while the water gently rose around their
bodies, for there were no waves, merely slight un-
dulations running on the surface, their caress perceptible only after they had passed. When Vanina
felt the cold, the sting, and the wet touch upon her
belly, even when she stood on tiptoe, she arched
her back against her will, and in spite of her distaste for heroics lifted her arms toward the sky as
if she were yielding herself a captive to some unexpected power and imploring mercy. How obdu-
rate, how monstrously callous it would have been
not to accord her, at least, her life!

So slight was the declivity that they walked on
for some time before the water reached their breasts.
They could easily distinguish pebbles against the
sand, as well as pieces of rusty iron, dead seaweed,
the pink spot of a sunken rag, a bloody flower they
would not have stepped on without distaste, and
they searched the bottom, thinking to find, perhaps,
a gold bracelet or some other treasure—but the poor
girls of Santa Lucia had no jewels except the rings
in their pierced ears and did not risk losing them
when they ventured into the sea. Vanina was still
holding her arms high in the air, her hands open,
fingers spread as if to release the nervous fluid

at the moment of self-surrender or of torture, and
she advanced without permitting her body to float,
for she knew that the bottom would slope up again,
and that they must cross a submerged shoal before
the water would be over their heads for good. The
cold was already no more than cool; the sea ran
between their legs like a huge sheet, wound about
their bodies, and uncoiled again in rhythm with
their breathing. They passed over the shoal bound-
ing the basin-shaped pool they disdainfully called
the "babies' bath," and then, both together, struck
out for the open sea.

Vanina, who had at once outdistanced her com-
panion by almost a length, noticed that the shore,
already distant, blurred behind her as she continued,
and that the bottom gradually fell away as well; she
was glad the movements of her arms and the con-
tinuous fluttering of her feet increased the sea's
depth beneath her with every moment. Glad too
that she could see ahead of her, around her, only
the brilliant horizon of the waves, she swam faster
and faster, feeling the water harden beneath her
belly and against her breast, hearing it hum in her
ears under the cap, smelling its violent perfume,
seizing it in her stiff palms and casting it behind
her, toward Juliette, with sovereign strokes. It was

not the least part of her happiness to realize that
she was thinking of nothing save her exertions of
the moment, her mind diminished, diluted until
she was conscious only of the effort her body was
making, its pure sensation. Prone as on a bed in
which she had buried her face, cradled in its oscil-
lations, her cheeks passed through the water, then
offered themselves to the sun, alternating fever and
frost as she turned her head.

She continued for several minutes which she
would again have found it difficult to account for
had some mythical and superhuman being (the goat-
footed witness) demanded it of her on pain of death.
But Pan is notoriously indulgent to those on whom
he has designs. The sun, suspended over the girl's
shoulders, shattered into crystal sparks the wave-
crests that ran from great distances toward her eyes,
their volume increased since she had reached the
open sea, sometimes lashing angrily against her
body, covering her cheeks with bitter foam. She
drank it down, but only to spit it up again; her
rhythm was broken, as if a screw had given somewhere, the breath came harder to her lungs, and
she grew conscious of her hammering heart; exhaustion weighed upon her, and the cold, suddenly
noticeable once more, made her tremble; yet proud

of her strength, she swam all the harder, only slightly slowing her strokes. Although she had never once looked back, she was sure of Juliette and had no doubt she was swimming close behind her like a faithful dog.

A moment later she heard someone cry out: "Vanina! Stop! We're too far out—the undertow will keep us from getting back."

"Far out," "undertow": magic words, like "gulf," "palm," "circus," "statue," "wizard," or "migratory"; words to penetrate the rubber cap and prompt the swimmer's drowsy memory restoring the sense of the past, the apprehension of the future. Vanina bent her knees in a scissors kick that sent half her body out of the great sparkling silk; arms raised, hands clasped, she subsided in a whirlpool of bubbles. Her eyes open despite the salt, she saw an arm churning in front of a pale shape that was Juliette's side, and surfaced next to her, piercing the sea's skin in a pirouette haloed with a thousand drops.

Then the two girls spoke of swimming in the simple terms appropriate when friends take such exercise together; they said the things pleasant to say when the sea is cold, when the sun is hot. They turned on their backs, and moving only the tips of their toes floated next to each other like sister ships that have lowered their sails, drifting together on a windless day.

Spread flat upon the sea, staring up into the sunlight, Vanina wondered—her body the union of these elements—where the knife dividing them would fall. Fire must be the stronger, for even though they lay within the water's embrace, their bodies barely grazing the surface, the swimmers were conscious only of the sun, a great disheveled wheel their dazzled eyes drew even closer than it was.

"The sun's going to charge us like a bull," Vanina said. "Hide, Juliette. He's heading for your red suit."

She herself was wearing only a suit of thin white material that went well with her brown skin. Two pieces of filmy cotton that did not keep her from feeling—or from looking—naked without overly offending the proprieties. And the sun played through the stuff as freely as if Vanina had been wearing gauze.

"Hide? Where?" said Juliette. "If you want, I'll take off my suit."

She slipped down one shoulder strap as far as her elbow, wriggled out of it, then freed the other arm, exposing her pale breasts to the brilliant air. She would have continued, pulling her suit entirely off, letting it sink to the bottom, if Vanina, wary of binoculars on shore (the carabiniers, like all police-men, were always on the prowl for innocence), had not begged her, laughing, to be more modest.

Together they giggled at this call to order and at the profligate gesture that had provoked it, and were happy as children, as kittens, only on a dry rug. The shore was very far away. Birds passed over-head, diving occasionally; they could see the downy bellies.

The moment came when once again they felt the cold, the water's weight and the effort it cost their arms to cast it behind them, their fingers merely to stay together. Vanina was the first to tire (as she had been, before, the first) and to admit it, as she was never second to be hungry, or thirsty, or sleepy, or in general to express any mutual desire. "Juliette is an animal," she told herself. She also told herself how much she liked her that way, how good it was to have an animal for a friend, a little heavier and a little stupider than oneself. For fun, in spite of their exhaustion (or to feel it still more) they decided to race one another back to the beach. Vanina let Juliette win: it was her due, as an animal. In the shallow water they coasted on their own momentum, their bodies lovely derelict hulls, content merely to flutter their feet now and then. The sandy bottom

ran against their breasts, their thighs. They grounded
less than a yard apart and rested, motionless, in
transparent pleasure.

Once out of the water, of course, it was even
hotter than before their swim. The cool relief that
clings to a wet skin lasted no more than three minutes and already they were completely dry, powdered with prickling salt. Juliette was spread-eagled
on her back; she had closed her eyes, savoring the
sun's heat, overpowered by the somnolence that is
to sleep what red is—or white—to black; but Vanina,
lying on her stomach beside her friend, in order to
struggle against this torpor which had lately cost
her painful awakenings and persistent burns, looked
about her, kept her mind alert (attentive to what
she saw), struggled to maintain her consciousness,
to augment it as much as possible by the contemplation of the slightest details. The sand, a uniform
desert for those who ask nothing of their eyes and
are satisfied with what the mere word for a thing
suggests ("sand" being one of the most banally per-
suasive of such words), spread in a series of almost
identical ridges, varying only in volume, all the way
to the dunes at the edge of the beach, and was alive
with tiny creatures that crept or flitted across it.
One species of diminutive shrimp- or horn-colored

shellfish occasionally ventured far from the moist
regions where it was found in greater numbers; it
plodded louselike along the sand, occasionally leaping into the air to escape a tiger beetle Vanina was
observing with inquisitive affection. She had noticed
similar beetles in Switzerland, but with bright green,
white-spotted wing cases instead of the iridescent
brown of this Mediterranean variety that nevertheless had the same white markings. Advancing by
sudden darts and short flights, the fierce little creature coursed along the furrowed sand; and when it
had seized a gnat or a sand flea in its mandibles, it
sucked the softer substance from its living victim
and then, with a jerk of its head, cast away the
drained shell. Vanina experimented with a fly, stun-
ning it and pulling off the wings in order to throw it
in front of the beetle, which immediately seized
the victim. Delighted by such voracity, the girl
hunted for other insects within reach—mosquitoes,
sand fleas, gnats—to use in the game she had invented, a sport as entrancing as falconry.

"Tiger beetles are handsome, predatory creatures," she thought. "I am helping the predatory
find their prey."

In order to collect enough victims for such car-
nage, Vanina turned to the right and to the left of

where she was lying, reached over the motionless
Juliette, burrowed in the sand like a child digging
a tunnel or a dog happily unearthing a bone. She
did not immediately notice the young man who had
stopped near by and was staring at her. When she
did, she stopped her game at first and pretended to
be watching the swimmers, slightly embarrassed,
at her age, to be caught playing like a little girl. For
the serious aspect of her sport had escaped her as
soon as she had seen herself through other eyes.

After a moment, during which she forced herself
to lie perfectly still, she glanced up again and saw
that the young man was still looking at her. But he
was looking at her without smiling at her, and that
was not what men did, as a rule. Doubtless he had
not stopped looking at her since his first glance. She
decided that he was handsome; she felt glad he was
watching her. She also realized that her game with
the tiger beetle involved a number of gestures be-
coming to her figure, and that she must look for
other flies, catch them, toss them into the air before
her at least for the sake of movement and in order
not to interrupt the performance, if not in behalf
of a game which had ceased to hold her interest.
That was how she would show him she was not

ashamed (although, of course, she had been) to play games while he was watching her.

Defiantly, she dared to crawl (though no more than a yard or so) toward him on all fours, knowing that her breasts had nothing to fear from the ordeal. She was excessive—as she had promised herself to be—and afterwards regretted having been so. He was still watching her, gravely.

She jostled Juliette who protested weakly, opened her eyes, and asked what time it was.

"Time to go," Vanina said, without taking her watch out of the bag. "Come on. I'm hungry."

She stood up, pulled her yawning friend to her feet, threw a beach robe over her shoulders, and pushed her ahead, following a few steps behind after having stopped to lace up her sandals.

When she passed the young man, what came into her head? Whatever occurred to her was so sudden, so unforeseen that she would not have been able to explain it, but: "Three o'clock this afternoon, in the pines below the village," she said to him, quickly bending down. "I'll be there." And she caught up with Juliette, who had noticed nothing.

Juliette and Vanina had taken lodgings with a
poor family of Siniscola whose house was more shed
than shelter: the early morning light showed through
the thatch and the girls were pleasantly surprised to
see, one stormy night, that the rain did not penetrate
it as well, either thanks to the roofer's skill or because the rain at Santa Lucia di Siniscola is as sparse
as it is sporadic. The girls slept in two narrow rooms
that had cost them a few thousand lire for the whole
summer. In the third, with scarcely room enough to
move between the bed, the cradle, the commode,
and the walls, lived Francesco Carone, a lobster
fisherman, with his wife Angela and their little
daughter. It was a rare occasion when Francesco
and Angela slept together, for the fisherman left
long before dawn to lift the traps dropped the day
before, and returned only late in the afternoon. If
they returned earlier, forced in by bad weather, the
traps stayed down and the village could count—at
best—on a handful of squids taken in the nets during
the first hours of daylight.

The Carones, like almost all the east-coast fishermen, were born on the island of Ponza (those on
the western coast are Ligurians, Catalans, or Nea-
politans), for the Sardinians are afraid of the sea,
or at least mistrust it, and abandon to foreigners the

trades that would make them venture out upon the water. Sometimes, before the Carones went to bed and the girls had not gone off somewhere (coming in late, they had to tiptoe through the first room so as not to wake the baby), they sat together gossiping on the doorstep. They discussed the gulls that the fisherman and his wife believed were souls in search of a body, coming to scream around the houses where there was a wedding bed or a body laid out for burial; and they mentioned certain toothless dogs, encountered only at night and supposedly hosts to souls in torment, that would take your hand in their cold, smooth mouths; they spoke of a great white skate that appeared on the surface of the sea and would vanish only after having heard the service for the dead chanted aloud by the crew; they discussed the eels that left the tide-pools during the heat of the day to couple with the snakes among the rocks of the beach; and they mentioned other serpents that tempted the goats to strange nuptials and made them give milk by biting their udders. It was rather fascinating to listen to such stories. Afterwards Vanina and Juliette would take a walk, for the nights in Sardinia are never very dark, or a drink at the harbor canteen where there was dancing.

They had landed at Olbia early in the morning a week ago. The calm was absolute on air and water alike, and a pure pinkish light fell across the reefs and islets scattered from one end of the bay to the other. Around them floated the unspoiled air, a splendor like a spell. They had let the crowd leave the white ship ahead of them, then Vanina, concentrating in some concern on the difficult maneuver, had headed the wheels of her little car (the "mousekin," she called it) down the gangway connecting the ship's garage with the pier. Once ashore they had been asked what strange caprice brought them to Sardinia, and the man at the filling station had strongly advised them to go home at once, and especially to avoid the southern part of the island, which he claimed was a nest of bandits. Vanina refused to listen to the man, who must have been from the north, or to Juliette, who was quite ready to admit her fears, and immediately headed south on a dusty, stony road in such disrepair that the mousekin, even at the lowest speeds, strained at every joint, vibrated from bumper to bumper, and made as much noise as a milk cart.

They had embarked at Civitavecchia the night before, having spent the day on the road from Bergamo. They had eaten lunch near Livorno, in a big whitewashed shed surrounded with barbed wire on which a single restaurant sign was posted. Some American soldiers, their trucks parked in front of the door, were being waited on by several rather pretty girls who received the new travelers none too politely. But after a long wait they were served bad spaghetti (overcooked, which is the Italian notion of how foreigners prefer it), red mullet drowned in oil and disguised in garlic and oregano, and a musky melon. Opposite them, a dark girl who was obviously naked under her rayon dress was gradually giving herself to the man next to her, a huge Negro who was stuffing rings of fried octopus in his mouth with one hand while the other was unfastening the zipper that opened her dress down one side from sleeve to stocking. The wine was black as ink and slightly acrid. The hair under the girl's arm was like an animal's. All in all, despite the bad food and the dirt, they were not sorry to have paid a visit to what was perhaps the "underworld" (in Vanina's opinion).

Vanina had had no difficulty obtaining permission to spend the summer vacation in Sardinia with Juliette. Her uncle and guardian, Count Marino Mari,

had given his leave almost at once. The little car
used for visiting the tenant farmers and the small
amount of money necessary for the trip were not
serious obstacles—scarcely matter for dicussion.
It was only the idea of such a journey itself that
had caused some comment. How the devil had
the girl thought of such a thing? "By chance," Vanina had answered, and she was not in the habit of
lying. Looking at the map, she had suddenly wondered about this huge island strayed so far from the
mainland, and then a friend had shown her some
earrings worn by the women there: gold loops each
with a teardrop pendant trembling beneath a pretty
filigree cock. Yes, the earrings, the cock especially,
had persuaded her she must see Sardinia.

Count Mari (whose coat of arms showed four
Saracen heads on a field vert—Sardinia has three,
Corsica one—and whose name might therefore be a
misreading of Mori) had never married; he lived
alone in the house of his ancestors, one of those
huge square yellow *palazzi* overloaded with marble
and supported by a colonnade around an interior
court that are an everyday marvel in the old cities
of northern Italy. Beneath ceilings painted with
clouds in false perspective and stuffed with cheru-
bim, in front of walls displaying friezes of twelve-

foot Nubians in colored stucco, prowled Count Mari, a stout man dressed in black, cane in hand, wearing a sort of tarboosh. Some of the marble had cracked; a smell of stone and urine rose from the courtyard on hot days and lingered in the great empty *salas*. For furniture there was nothing but an infrequent chair, a broken prie-dieu, a few tables on which could be seen the traces of cocoons, and some long horsehair *banquettes* the count would throw himself on when he felt sleepy, after meals. His niece, especially since she had not come alone from Bergamo, was keeping him from digesting in peace. And he did not like the dust raised, the *palazzo*'s silence broken by steps other than his own or those of the one valet who had served him for many years.

Juliette Combourgeois happened to be in Vanina's class at the school in Lausanne where both girls, with an indolence neither bothered to dissimulate, were "finishing their studies," and was her best friend as well (in a manner of speaking, for Vanina prided herself in secret on never having had—promising herself never to have—a close friend). The fact is that they went to films together frequently, or visited the pink- and green-shuttered *patisseries* to eat rich pastry (Juliette greedily, Vanina not with-

out a certain lassitude). And they took walks along
the lake at Ouchy, Juliette allowing herself to be
dragged along by Vanina, who was bored with the
younger girls and interested in a swan. In the habit,
therefore, of making decisions and being obeyed,
the Italian girl had invited her Swiss friend to spend
the vacation with her in her own country.

It would be idle (although, of course, not impossible) to begin even earlier in time; yet where, once
you turn back (and you have started telling a story),
can you stop? Everything connects, and however
scrupulously I should examine what was being delivered eighteen years previously from the womb of
Countess Lidia Mari, Count Marino's sister-in-law
who died with her husband during the bloody events
which enliven the history of postwar Italy but which
I do not wish to concern myself with (now), you
would still not be sufficiently well informed about
the heroine of my story: the *Contessina* Vanina.
Basta, then. It is enough that she had very large
eyes as dark as black pansies, eyes which give me
every excuse for dreaming. . . . Vanina's adventure
begins at Santa Lucia di Siniscola, when she makes
her way to the little pine grove behind the village,
at three o'clock in the afternoon.

She had left the house by her window (straddling
the bar across its lower half), without a word to
Juliette, asleep in the next room; daily naps had
become a habit in Santa Lucia, where their spirits
languished after dinner, burdened by the heat and
the strong wine. Juliette would not be disturbed if
she awakened before Vanina's return ánd found her
gone, for even at school Vanina was in the habit of
running off alone, without the slightest explanation
—escapades so rudely denied to those who occasionally tried to accompany her that they lost all interest
in asking a second time. Sitting on the ground at the
foot of the wall, she took off her espadrilles and
shook out the sand, then put them on again, knotting
the black laces higher to accentuate the quite aston-
ishing delicacy of her ankle (easily encircled by her
thumb and forefinger) and the arching line of her
calf. Then she walked around the house and left
the sandy alley, passing in front of the church across
the cropped, scorched grass where nets were drying
among the lobster pots the women would mend and
the rusty iron poles lying where they had been
dropped; the children would pick them up later to
play with, beating each other and risking tetanus
from the dirt contaminated by rotten fish guts.

The shadow of the church, the only building ex-

cept the carabiniers' barracks that showed above the
low houses, began to darken the ground, but Vanina
continued walking directly into the sun; her eyes
were not yet accustomed to its brightness and hurt
her. She kept them fixed on the ground to avoid
the lobster shells and other garbage that had been
thrown there. When she looked up she saw the pale
pink stucco of the church, crumbling with age, and
the dark niches, more bestial than human, formerly
reserved for pilgrims; she saw the sky's violent blue
and felt as if she were walking into fire. "Why did I
leave?" she wondered, and decided that nothing in
the world could make her turn back now. Although
she did not know what she was heading for, she
asked herself nothing about it.

The village was absolutely deserted this early in
the afternoon. The able-bodied men were at sea
(who knows if they too were not napping in the
boats?), and everyone else had withdrawn behind
closed shutters. The miserable shops, where earth's
loveliest fruits rotted next to dirty ribbons, smelly
pomades, and boxes of dissolving candy, were
closed; the tobacco shop, which had the only license
to sell salt, was closed; the shutters at the windows
of the carabiniers' barracks were closed. Even the
dogs had disappeared, and not one was barking,

though when anyone passed this way by night there
were furious howls at each door.

It was as if even the plants were asleep, for the
boughs laden with little white flowers, a variety of
jasmine that nightly perfumed the air around the
church, withdrew their fragrance during the heat
of the day, as if not to bestow it vainly, in the absence of men. Vanina picked a cluster and rubbed
it between her fingers to recover the missing odor.
Then she fastened it in her hair, near the nape of
her neck. It occurred to her—for she despised priests
—that it was from growing on these walls that the
flowers had learned such base economy, of which
they were fortunately ignorant wherever they grew
wild. Any priest's garden, somewhere else, would
have disabused her, yet her error makes her youthful
fanaticism no less appealing, especially her con-
temptuous snort, like a headstrong filly's, as she
passed the church.

From neither sea nor mountain came the slightest
breath of air (and the fishermen, she reminded herself, might be becalmed until tomorrow morning).
After having passed the church she took another
alley that led out of the village, leading downhill a
little and following the coast. Grass would not grow
here, vanquished by the salt's infiltration, and Va-

nina sank down into sand and into dust finer than
sand, which would have filled the air if the wind
had risen. Her espadrilles grew heavy again; she
decided not to empty them, not wanting to stop
every other minute; she regretted not having put on
her open sandals instead, the ones she had worn
this morning to the beach. The farther she walked
along this alley, the poorer and more precarious the
houses became, and Vanina glanced about a little
apprehensively, although she had already remarked
such windows and their curious frames: stripes of
the rawest blue conceivable or possible in paint, and
less frequently of brilliant pink, bordered with white
or pale gray, brushed on a rough wall around a
square hole or a black or dark-red shutter. Like a
tattoo around a wound dressed by someone more
expert in spells than surgery, such signs, Signora
Carone had told her, were to ward off the flies. Certainly the need was great, for ever since an immense
amount of insecticide had been spread or sprayed
over the whole island in the praiseworthy attempt
to destroy all malaria-bearing mosquitoes, the flies
had modified certain characteristics of their species
(to their advantage); the generations produced from
those that had survived the poison, virtually a new
variety after the others had perished, were extremely

prolific, much hardier than their ancestors, and hair-
ier, noisier, greedier, and more aggressive as well.
Man's only hope was that they might be afraid of
raw blue or pink. "Heaven's colors—and the church's
too, except the church is paler because it is old,"
Vanina thought, her eyes still fierce with scorn.

As she reached the last houses and was passing
a shed roofed with reeds and stones, she heard a
series of rather ferocious grunts. In spite of the heat,
no one was sleeping here. She pushed open the
shutter which was not bolted, and looked inside.
It was a stable and in it was a single, fat, powerful
hog, standing on its hind legs, its snout wedged into
the window-recess. He was very black, like all his
breed in Sardinia, which are more closely related to
the boar than to the domestic pig, and even had
two tiny tusks around which the upper lip was
tucked. This must have been the stud hog of Santa
Lucia, for a repulsive smell emanated from the shed,
and the beast was housed in more space and solitude
than it would otherwise have received. Soon daunted
by the overpowering stench, Vanina gently closed
the shutters on the creature's snout, yet somehow,
from the contemplation of this great black hog
sprawling in its own filth and apparently waiting
for something (what?), she had sensed, suddenly,

within herself a kind of tenderness, deep and almost
fraternal—she had felt a certain inhuman happiness
that she would not attempt to elucidate. She had
forgotten all about the "church's colors," the cause
of her earlier irritation, and continued at a good
pace, regarding heaven and earth alike with friendly
eyes.

Soon she was beyond the village without ever
having noticed just when she had left the buildings
behind, glad not to see any more houses around her,
not to be guided any more by walls; spellbound by
the sun that struck at her bare head with its dazzling
spears. The blood pounded along the arteries in
her temples, and she inhaled the sea air deeply, its
immense purity making her forget the odors of men
and beasts. The sea was on her left, below the path,
still as a pond, pale and brilliant, free of all sails, all
smoke; on her right was the pine grove, like another
darker sea of shining oxide green, the froth rigid
upon it in the absence of the slightest breath of air.
Strands of barbed wire surrounded the grove to protect the young trees against the village goats, but
Vanina knew such entanglements reached no farther
than the next creek, and that there was no need to
tear her skirt or dirty herself trying to thread her
way among the rusty points.

She climbed down by a short, steep path, a sandy outflow where roots came to the aid of hands and feet (the pines at the grove's edge, their roots half unearthed, looked as though they had been planted on the backs of great, gnarled spiders), and reached the sea where it ran up on a beach of pebbles and low rocks. The very ones where, according to the gossip she had heard, a fisherman had surprised an eel and a serpent mating in the blaze of noon; if this was indeed the place, it would be wiser to abandon it straightaway, for the serpent would have attacked any man or woman foolhardy enough to spy on its unnatural union. Vanina hurried on, glancing at the red and jagged stones where the mosses looked like brown hair at the bottom of the little pools. Crabs were doubtless hidden there, but nothing moving could be seen, and there was neither sign nor shadow of either fish or reptile.

At the other end of the bay, marked by a maze of darker rocks and bluish pebbles lying upon them like great eggs, the path gradually mounted again toward the pine grove.

She had to pierce a curtain of tamarisks, parting their silky branches (which at nightfall exuded a dew as salty as tears, she remembered as she passed).

The woods, of course, were as empty as the vil-

lage streets, the fields, the vineyards, the beach, and
—for so it seemed—the world itself at this time of
day; but not empty with the same innocence. They
were like a prison that might have been a trap as
well, where you might at any moment be assailed
from any side. The nature of a woods is to be enclosed at the same time that it is laid open in every
direction, because of the thousands of trunks, the
tens or hundreds of thousands sometimes, that sur-
round you like palings planted to hold you captive,
and because of the multifarious openings between
them through which an aggressor could easily steal,
but which form a labyrinth that keeps you from
escaping.

"When the maiden entered the woods, the stranger came to seize her"—Vanina listened curiously to
this little sentence that hummed in her ears though
she had done nothing to summon it, born in the
state of mental vacuity that had been hers as she
walked along beneath the sun, a state which had
given way to an almost feverish agitation of spirit
the moment she found herself in the shade of the
branches. "The stranger came to seize her"—yes; and
was that not the very reason she had stolen from her
room? Yet she saw no one, and immediately decided
he was not there, he would not come, he was sleep-

ing like some animal—like everyone else—and she
would wander alone in the woods until nightfall. She
thought she might go mad, perhaps it would be *la
follia* that would come to meet her, a great, pure
white thing that would embrace her and efface her
until she lost her mind.

She walked on, listening to the sound of her own
steps. Her feet (she had emptied her espadrilles after
all, at the end of the sandy path) made a sliding
noise on the pine needles that carpeted the ground,
it sounded like a gasp—faint but audible very far
away, for in the woods silence is only a word; or
rather, an echo chamber, so that a thousand tiny
sounds reached Vanina's ears that she would have
hardly noticed in open country. There was the whir-
ring and chafing of wing-cases, the droning of grass-
hoppers or locusts (these last none too frequent, a
recent storm having drowned many of their number), the movements of a squirrel or a bird leaping
from one branch to another, of a snake or a lizard
making its way to shelter, and the creaking of sun-
scorched wood like the noises made by furniture
at night, which are said to be the work of ghosts
in haunted houses. She stopped, leaned her cheek
against a young pine bole, pressed hard against the
rough bark from which several flakes rose, ready

to drop off. The odor of pitch filled her throat, mastered her with surprising brutality after the deceptive sweetness of the balsam, but it was too late to defend herself. She noticed the pattern of the bark printed on the skin of her arm; so it was the same —perhaps in bolder relief—on her face. "I am disfigured," she thought. But what difference did it make, as long as she was alone in the woods? Besides, the marks disappeared immediately.

She heard someone walking in a part of the woods she could not see, to her right. She stood perfectly still and then, when the steps (and the sliding noise) stopped, began to walk in their direction. It was impossible to see more than ten or twelve yards, the pines grew so thickly, it was dark beneath their branches, the grove's edge was far behind her, and once again the little sentence hummed in Vanina's ears. When she stopped, the steps immediately began again, and were not far off when she stopped hearing them. It was her turn to move, according to the rules of the game (which she accepted, even though this was the first time she had played and had never been taught what they were). All she had to do was walk a little farther, slip between several tree trunks, and she found herself in front of the young man from the beach, who was waiting for her. When he saw her he threw down his cigarette and Vanina stepped on it to keep the woods from catching fire. He smiled, showing his teeth, and she smiled back, without the slightest embarrassment. The meeting had taken place. It had happened as simply as a sunrise.

"I'm glad you have come," she said.

He did not seem affronted or even surprised by her immediate use of the intimate Italian form. Looking at her with insistence and concern, as if he were estimating the worth of a costly object, or a sculptor deciding what he could make of a model, he said: "I'm glad too. You are adorable. There's no other word."

In truth, whether or not he was trying to flatter her, he was not deceiving her. The girl, not tall, though certainly not too short, lifted the perfect oval of her face to look at him more closely, and beneath the mass of her dark hair, drawn back into a great, soft bun, it was her eyes especially that delighted him—wide, enormous, globed slightly beyond the curve of her face and victorious in their wager to set the night's profundity with the glitter of polished stone. The mouth was arched without being wide, modeled by (or for) the pleasure of the senses, but with a mocking or wayward expression, and the teeth gleamed. There is something particularly *present* (in relation to time) in a lovely smile, though certain persons cannot see teeth without being reminded of death. Everything opposed this notion, moreover, in Vanina's face, which was the very type of youth and life, smooth and fleshy like a magnolia petal. The temples were broadly rounded, and if upon them formed—as at the armpits—several beads of perspiration, this was merely the flaw in the armor, the indispensable defect in any woman's beauty, perceived just in time to restore the observer's courage, to make a man of him again. The nose was small and thin, in accord with the mockery of the lips; the ears so small as to have a kind of monstrous perfection (no contradiction between these two words!).

Vanina's feet were almost bare, resting on the heelless rope soles; her legs were bare. She wore only a sleeveless, almost shapeless, linen dress, a kind of tunic scalloped more deeply in back than at the throat, but of an unimaginable red. The color exploded in the shadow of the undergrowth and dressed the girl in fire, like the flames of a witch's stake.

"Come," he said, taking her by the hand. "I want to take you to a place where I will see you better."

She yielded to his request, and they walked on together among the pines, bending—the boy especially
—to avoid the dead branches that in this section of
new growth were particularly thick and low. It was
strange—Vanina congratulated him upon it and herself as well, in her heart—that they remained silent
after these first few words, that neither one of them
laughed aloud. But a forest, a woods, more than
temples or tombs, has a massive character from
which it is not easy to escape. Had it not been for
the trees, certainly, they would have been less serious.

Soon she saw where he had wanted to lead her.
The place was like a great basin in the sandy earth
which the roots had kept from blowing away, where
the pines—sparser here—had grown much higher and
more vigorously than elsewhere. A little moss had
sheathed the trunks at their base, a tough grass had
appeared among the dry needles in the low places,
and there were even little pink and fleshy plants,
pressed flat against the ground, that bore spathes of
tiny flowers. The place was incomparably fresh, as
young as if it had been created the night before, or
as if no one had ever set foot in it. Vanina had not
let go of her guide's hand, which was a firm support
for her upon the slippery needles, especially when

it came time to descend into this region of trembling light.

He seized her by the wrists (the little sentence, within her, had been silent since their meeting) and placed her, but gently, with her back against a tree. He stood before her and looked at her, without smiling. She looked at him in the same way. His forehead was high, the black hair curling round it like a fringe, too long elsewhere and trailing down the nape of his neck. His eyes were dark and shining under the strongly arched brows, his nose thin and slightly aquiline, his chin large, his mouth severe. "I know who he looks like," Vanina said to herself. "He's a painting by Giorgione in flesh and blood: the young man whose portrait I loved so much in the Old Pinacothek." She also reminded herself that this was just the sort of comparison to avoid, like all references to *objets d'art*, if she ever tried, one day, to tell her story. She wondered how he would look in a fur jacket: "In winter, in foxskins, how handsome he would be . . . I wonder what he's going to do."

As if in answer, he made a gesture that brought her closer to his chest. It is quite probable he was going to kiss her. But she freed herself with a quick movement, an ease that left him crestfallen.

"Sit down," she said to him, first sitting down herself.

And before he had opened his mouth (though he did not seem very talkative), she hurled a flood of words upon him, yet somehow in order, thoughts rising to meet the words without her understanding anything of what was happening, or opening, within herself, without her being able to hold her speech in check to the slightest degree. These words were completely unforeseen, completely scandalous. She would have been horribly shocked to have heard them spoken by one of her schoolmates, or Juliette —even yesterday.

"Ti voglio bene"—she had begun by telling him that. Then she told him, without hesitating or low-ering her eyes, that she loved him (which is the same thing, said with a completer, deeper consent), but that she did not want to risk losing her head and yielding to a momentary confusion. That she wanted, yes, to be his with no restriction, but still following her own instincts and being quite con-scious of what she was doing, remaining capable of seeing into herself as into clear water. Not today, for she needed a long time to think about what was going to happen between herself and the man she loved (for she did love him, she was not ashamed

to say so again). First of all, then, she would make a *retreat*. And the next night (or more exactly: after the next evening), he might expect her between twelve-thirty and one, on the beach, beyond the little canal by which the sea communicated with the sound and its fisheries. She would come to meet him. And he was not to smile at her detailed instructions, or make fun of the rendezvous she was arranging for him one after the other, for she had never had any before, with a man. It was her habit and her taste to take everything seriously; she was not going to treat love lightly.

She told him that he should be careful and, above all, that he should avoid frivolity, for he had a handsome, grave face, like those you could see in the old paintings, in museums. That he should keep that dark look of his, and that he should listen carefully to what she still had to say. Not a single arrangement of their mutual delight must fail or falter, once that delight had begun; therefore it must be organized now, down to its smallest details, like a ballet contrived for a king and a queen. If she refused to accept a surprise embrace here, then with all the more reason she would not allow him to strip from her there a consent she had already accorded unrestrictedly, provided its clauses were respected. It was in subjection that she wished to give herself to him; a queen, yes, but a captive queen, a prisoner, a slave submissive to everything out of pure caprice. Thus, when she would come to meet him at the water's edge, he was to seize her somewhat brutally, and bind her hands behind her back. After all, he could spare her a necktie in such a cause!

She said that she wanted to give him the greatest pleasures in the world, far more than the whores in bordellos and the adulterous wives who had doubtless been his bedfellows had given him up to now. For this reason she begged him not to take her unawares, once he had bound her, not to take her carelessly, too quickly, since she would have come there only to be taken by him on the sand, and she knew quite well beforehand to what she would be exposed. She wanted him to amuse himself with her —to caress her a little beneath her clothes before drawing them from her body. Perhaps she would be wearing shorts, to offer him from the first her legs bare to the thigh. Or a full skirt. Who could say how she would be dressed?

But he must not touch her before the night and the time she had chosen for their pleasure.

And then, he must know this too: she was a virgin. No, he must not speak; silence was very becom-

ing to him. There was no need for him to tell her
his name, at least during the first days. She had no
reason to know the name of the man she loved. For
Vanina, he would be the young man from the beach,
the young man from the pine grove. Wasn't that
better than Fabrizio, or Frederico?

Now they would separate; but before going she
would make him one more promise. This very night
she would show herself to him. After eleven o'clock
he might come—without making any noise—to the
house she was staying in with her friend—the fisherman's cottage painted pink and blue, behind the
restaurant. Her window was the one facing the pine
grove; there were no others on that side of the
house, no chance of a mistake. The shutters would
be closed but not bolted, and could be opened from
outside by a mere push. Then he would see her. But
under no pretext must he enter her room.

When she had finished speaking she stood up,
rested her hand on his shoulder a moment, and ran
away. Like a man drinking from whom the water is
snatched away, he called her back, shouting, "Vanina," spellbound by this sinuous name she had left
him as a pledge, though she had refused to hear the
sound of his own. But she did not answer, running
off with great leaps, so fast that to overtake her now

was unthinkable. She had already climbed up the slope of dry needles, crossed the ridge, and was plunging off under the branches. The sound of her steps died away. With neither joy nor sadness, with a certain indifference, in fact, the way one feels, sometimes, in the best and worst of love, he lowered his eyes to the ground. In front of him, near his foot, one of the little fleshy plants formed a five-pointed star on the gray earth. He gazed at it; it swelled until it filled his whole field of vision, while his thoughts drowned him in a kind of sleek, gleaming water that was Vanina.

The girl, as soon as she had decided she was out of danger, had stopped running so desperately. She listened: not a sound. He had obeyed her, then, and had not left the hollow, in accordance with her desire. She felt a desire still more violent, which was to be back in her room. To reach it as soon as possible, she crossed the entire length of the woods instead of turning toward the sea. Once beyond the pines, she was stopped by the strands of barbed wire, but slipped under them, in the dust, at a place which must have been dug out on purpose, for a path led directly to it from the village. It was not difficult to pass through, even (or especially) for a nanny-goat. The first houses of the village were a few steps away. She hurried on, paying no attention to anything in the streets, without seeing the few people that were beginning to come and go.

Something had changed inside her, collapsed, vanished perhaps, yet she did not recognize the metamorphosis and failed to grow indignant at its signs. The speech (scarcely reconcilable with the modesty that hitherto had been her casual principle) delivered in the pine grove had somehow transformed her character (instead of having been formed by it), and without having desired such a thing, without even being aware of it, she had completely assumed the mien of the singular maiden who had uttered it. More simply: she had become body and soul the girl who would be surrendered to the stranger in the night to come, after tomorrow, and she felt the weight of her bonds, self-assured and curious to know how the other would play his part.

She returned as she had left (there was a most convenient log beneath the window), and threw herself down on her bed without uncovering it or undressing. In the next room, Juliette was still resting.

Later, the Swiss girl pushed open the door (which

a stone on the floor kept shut in the absence of any lock) and said, "I slept well, did you? Did you dream?"

"I don't think so," Vanina answered.

After the dinner, after the nap, it was again time
for the afternoon swim when they took the path to
the beach. Already there (but clustered on the first
reaches, near the pebbly strand where the boats
were drawn up, while the rest of the shore, a little
farther on, remained deserted), were all the inhabitants of Santa Lucia who were not working and not
too afraid of the sun: boys, girls, mothers still young
already surrounded by herds of children, a few old
people who treated their rheumatism by having
themselves buried in the burning sand. There were
also the foreigners who had summer houses or who
rented a room from some villager to spend the vacation here, and if most were Sardinians—families from
Olbia or Nuoro, or from Sassari, or even Cagliari
—some, an extremely small number, were "mainlanders" (as they were called), particularly penniless
students attracted by, and limited to, the island's
low prices. The young man from the pine grove
probably belonged to the latter breed, for his accent,
in the few words Vanina had permitted him, was
like that of Pisa and Florence.

It was no disappointment to Vanina that he was
not in the sea today, or on the sand. On the contrary,
she preferred thinking that he had remained in the
woods after she left him, sitting on the ground near

the tree beneath which she had spoken to him for so long, and that he was meditating on what he had heard. Never in his life—young as he was, scarcely nineteen or twenty—could he have heard such words, and he had obviously been bewildered by them, since he had not attempted to reply or even disobey. He had recovered, of course, later on, perhaps he was kissing the tree trunk now, or he was dreaming about what the evening held in store for him. Love is not a common thing on which embellishments may be hung, Vanina thought. It must be offered and accepted, given and received, in that spirit of simplicity and ardor which is the best way of reaching an intimacy between bodies and between souls.

Vanina and Juliette walked along the water's edge (they preferred mornings for swimming, afternoons for walking under the slanting sun, mixing with the villagers, keeping in shade or solitude, sitting when they liked and chattering idly, as they did at school); they might have thought themselves in the lobby of a music-hall during intermission. The foreign girls, city-bred, were doubtless little different from girls on all the bathing beaches in the world, but if some women and girls of Santa Lucia owned real bathing suits—quite chaste, in obedience to the curé's instructions: sporting a skirt that began at the waist

and cut to show as little décolleté as possible without
being too ridiculous—the others, in the old fashion,
went into the water in long shifts of white or sometimes flowered cotton. When they came out, of
course, the light cloth that clung to their bodies and
their breasts that were stiffened by the cold exposed
them to all eyes in an accentuated state of nudity
far more indecent than mere nakedness. Vanina
stared with pleasure at these girls: several among
them, the youngest, were outrageously beautiful,
the hard points of their breasts protruding from a
dark aureole, their round bellies balanced on strong
thighs, their black triangles like the brand of the
herd. She pointed them out to Juliette, who could
only laugh, embarrassed, overcivilized; Vanina
would have liked to show them to the young man
from the woods—he would not have laughed at such
displays consecrated by the sun and the sea's salt,
for he had not laughed or even smiled when she had
made her speech to him, which was after all nothing
but a young fanatic's vow of violent impurity. She
decided that the brutal shamelessness of these girls
was the admirable fruit of shame itself; and that she
could follow the same passage in reverse from defilement to purity. "It is because I am a virgin," she
told herself, "that I want to be bound in order to be

riven. Will I suffer much? I still have that odor of resin at the back of my throat!"

Fearful of being discovered in the throes of the passion that was choking her, Vanina glanced at Juliette and found her staring back. No, she had understood nothing: she was waiting, as was her custom, for Vanina to decide which direction to take, toward the pines or along the sea, and in anticipation took her pleasure (as she called it in her naïve Swiss way) in the bright sun, the warm air, as she might have done on the shores of a lake.

"Let's go," Vanina said. "Those girls give me a headache—they think they have to scream whenever they get in the water. If God loved me like the prophet Elisha, I would ask him to send not bears but sharks, and the worst kind too—that would shut them up. Have you noticed that the ones who scream the loudest and wave their arms the most are the ones wearing the bathing suits? The others keep still, like women of antiquity. Look at those great wild beauties—so calm under the wet cloth . . ."

"They keep still because they're ashamed," Juliette said.

Vanina decided not to contradict her, for she scorned being in the right, or in the wrong, and had not invited her friend to Sardinia for the sake

of argument, which she found tiresome; but she was
nonetheless convinced that Juliette, for all her good
sense, had misjudged again—if there was any shame
or embarrassment among the bathers, it was certainly accountable to those who screamed and wriggled at the touch of the waves, while the others who
stayed squatting in the tepid shallows until the sea
began to grow cold about them, then rose slowly
out of the water, concealing nothing, felt no more
shame than heifers, thought no more of modesty
than mares.

The farther they walked the fainter the girls'
screams grew behind them, and the stronger in
their stead became the cries of gulls and pipers
that were squabbling nearby, on a sandbar where
they had gathered in great numbers.

"The souls are upset today, apparently," said
Juliette. "Would you ask God to send you a hawk
to get rid of them, or an osprey with big mustaches
of red hair between its toes?"

"Heretic! You're as incapable of adoration as you
are of love! If I believed I was loved by a god, or
loved one, I'd tear off my clothes right now and
swim unflinching through a sea of sharks to give
myself to him—like those Polynesian girls who threw
themselves naked into the sea, with only red flowers

in their hair, to meet the ships carrying white men who perhaps were gods to them, and who would wed them, brutally, after the manner of gods. They would swim far out to sea in search of such men, and they sang when they saw the sails. The sailors tossed down ropes and drew them out of the water like big shiny fish, and took them, roughly, over a coil of rope or on the boards of the deck. I do not think the sailors loved them, they were only vulgar men, deprived of women for a long time, and when they saw a necklace or a bracelet of pearls they took it in exchange for a string of worthless beads or a blow of the fist, and sometimes they threw the girls back into the sea, exhausted as they were after submitting to so many men. But *they* were lovers, those girls. And for that reason nothing could discourage them, and if they managed to reach land, the stories they told persuaded their younger companions to put fresh flowers in their hair and run naked into the sea, to be robbed and raped and murdered in their turn by the white gods, when the signal came that the ships were near."

"I wouldn't have gone to meet those boats," said Juliette. "And if I had a pearl—a black pearl, my favorite kind—it would take more than a god to get it away from me." She played with the ring on her

forefinger, a heavy gold loop set with as many colored stones as a rose window, which she had bought
from a priest in Siniscola; she had become jealously
attached to it when the old man told her it had been
among his church relics for more than a century.
Offered to the Madonna in gratitude for some par-
don or other, it could nevertheless be sold for the
needs of such a poor parish as this, and would protect the woman who possessed it until the Madonna
appeared in her dreams to ask it back again—for the
ring still belonged to God. In which case it would
be wise to return the ring to the church's treasury
at once; without compensation, of course, for there
would be as much merit in this action as glory in
the dream. The priest had added that after having
adorned many women for varying periods of time
and brought all of them luck, the jewels of the Madonna almost always returned to her in the end.

In spite of the beauty of the ring (which the priest
had taken out of a filthy handkerchief in order to
offer it to them), Vanina regarded it with something
like anxiety, if not repugnance, and would have
preferred it not to leave the church (or the curé's
pocket). Sometimes she asked her friend: "Did you
dream about the Madonna?"

Invariably Juliette would assure her she had not.

And it was clear that under no pretext would she return the ring—not for anything in the world.

As they talked they had drawn nearer the birds, several of which flew off at their approach, then all the rest together; the girls discovered that what had attracted them were some scraps of meat or fish abandoned on the beach, not thrown far enough for the sea to wash them away. A family party had settled down here, a clan that must have come from one of the mountain villages where life had not changed from one century to the next, and such garbage was doubtless the remains of their meal that the wasps as well were working at. Tarpaulins, worn carpets slung between the wheels of a cart, and some stakes on which rush matting had been hung provided a precarious shelter, but one that sufficed for summer, where the women rested in the shade, covered with long shawls. Some children were chasing one another, all stark naked; one, who seemed to be a little girl, was rolling in the sand while the others whipped her with fronds of dried seaweed tied to sticks; she groaned but did not try to run away. There was no man in sight except for one half-grown boy behind the encampment, watering a horse in the black wastes of the sound. He was riding bareback, with no more clothes on than the

children, and from time to time he dug his heels
into the horse's flanks to force him into the water
that reached no farther than the animal's belly. The
boy's hair was rather long and fell down over one
cheek when he turned back. He was singing as he
spurred on his steed, the song a simple tune repeated many times, its notes very shrill and not out
of harmony with the reeds drooping over the soot-
colored water, the cattle lying under the oaks on the
other side of the marsh, nor with his own brown,
adolescent body firmly astride the skittish horse
that soon grew calmer in the cool water.

The birds circled above the sea without flying
too far from their little wave-lapped peninsula. The
approach of human beings had chased them, but
they would return to forage there as soon as the
girls were far enough away to be harmless. Their
cries tore the air with shrill sounds like small, white
flames, while the sun moved down the sky toward
the mountain ridges, and the sand turned pink; later
it would change to gray and then to violet before
melting into the darkness; such cries were strangely
modulated, in the same key as the boy's song, as if
the young horseman's voice had given them the
pitch, the dominant tone. Certain moments, in places
far away from cities, modern buildings, and what is

generally called "civilization," reveal to a sensitive
witness an extraordinary harmony (more apparent,
of course, than real), in which it seems as though all
the elements of nature are in accord. The witness,
according to his character, more often than taking
part in it, has the sense of being excluded from this
play of correspondences. So he develops a feeling
for solitude that enforces a mistrust of others quite
as much as the tedium—or the pleasure—of being
alone. Vanina thought of her rendezvous that evening, of the much more grave and consequential one
she would go to the following night, and all at once,
confronted so closely with the future she had chosen
for herself, grew frightened.

Turning to Juliette in a sudden need for com-
panionship, if not yet for confidence, she pointed to
the rider staring at them across the reeds. He had
rested his fist on the top of his thigh, either to conceal his genitals or to indicate them to better effect.
"What do you think of that boy?" she asked. "Isn't
he handsome?"

"The young savage?" Juliette replied. "I think he
belongs in the landscape, but it's hardly a picture
to my taste—or yours, I should think!"

There was no use pointing out to Juliette that she
knew nothing of Vanina's tastes, since these had

betrayed themselves only so recently, fastening on
an object she could not keep out of her thoughts—
proudly sometimes, greedily, joyously, timidly, fear-
fully now, but always passionately. As for Juliette's
tastes, the girl herself let it be understood that they
need not be imperious for her to give herself quite
readily to some student—preferably a stranger—encountered in a *patisserie*, the possessor of a roomy
car or a motorboat good for reaching the middle of
the lake quickly, supposedly for a sunbath, and if
she was probably exaggerating this facility of hers,
she was not inventing it. Girls too, dormitory friends,
had experimented agreeably enough with this readi-
ness of hers. Availability was one of Juliette's virtues,
according to the gossip of Lausanne. Vanina, who
despised the girl more than she admired or envied
her for this accomplishment, but who would have
been glad to see her at grips with a man, who had
in fact invited her for the summer with something
of this voyeur's intention in mind, regretted (feeling
somehow cheated) that her friend was so indifferent
to the naked young horseman.

"He's very handsome," she said. "Savage or not,
if I loved him, I would not be ashamed to have him
take me on his horse and carry me off anywhere,
in front of you and everyone else."

"Then it's a good thing you don't love him," said
Juliette calmly.

Vanina angrily bit the inside of her cheek until
she tore the membrane and tasted blood. She had
been on the point of telling Juliette that she loved
someone else, who was much handsomer than this
boy, someone who looked like one of the most beautiful portraits ever painted (though Juliette, for all
her pretensions, knew nothing about painting), and
that this very night he would see her as a man is not
often permitted to see a girl, and that the following
night she would yield herself to him so that he would
bind her and make use of her as he liked. But had
she spoken such things aloud, she would now be
wanting to tear out her tongue; she declared herself
guilty and deserving of punishment for coming so
close to revealing her thoughts. For Juliette would
have understood absolutely nothing, and it was perfectly ridiculous even to dream of taking her for a
confidante. Solitude, on reflection, was not so frightening, and might even be considered as a state of
grace in her particular case, in view of the fact that
love was her cause and filled her whole being. She
wondered if she would still feel alone, when she
would be imprisoned in the young man's arms,
against his chest; she wondered if love was not more

of a marvel when it was received in solitude. Her
fears had vanished. She decided she had been wrong
to be afraid at all, since she had been well assured
of being made for love, as the fish is made for water
and the bird for air, as the salamander, according to
the ancient adepts, is made for fire.

"What are you thinking about?" Juliette asked,
suddenly putting her arm around Vanina's waist.
"Why are you so quiet? You're not angry?"

No, she was not angry. On the contrary: Juliette's
blindness to a thing as disturbing as a handsome
naked boy riding bareback in a marsh, her heaviness
of spirit, a certain practicality that weighed her
down, everything, in fact, that made her different
Vanina now accepted with immense indulgence and
great affection. She did not say so, of course, nor did
she speak any more about her earlier thoughts, but
humored her friend with compliments she might
have bestowed on a favorite pet, responded to her
caresses, and hurried on, drawing Juliette with her.

At the sea's edge (for walking was easier on the
wet sand) they found a big sea-urchin the waves
were washing back and forth along the beach.
Larger than two fists together, almost spineless now,
and pink, it had precisely the shape of a heart as
Vanina pulled it out of the water. She broke it open

with a kick to see what it was like inside. Once burst, it showed only some dark reddish entrails smelling violently of rot.

"What are you doing?" Juliette asked.

"Giving the souls something to eat. It's the kind of food they like best. You'll see—they'll be here as soon as we go."

And they walked on, as much to escape the stench as to leave the birds free to feast on the guts in peace.

In a little while they reached the fisheries, but did not cross the narrow channel through which a rather strong current was flowing from the sound, for it was near the time of the low tide. Walking at the channel's edge, they approached a structure that looked like a gold-washing machine or the remains of some fortification on piles; on closer examination it turned out to be a triangular weir built of stakes, flat rocks, and planks, with an opening at the vortex on the principle of a lobster pot, so that fish could enter the sound from the sea and were prevented from leaving it. A trap, then; Vanina thought they might put something of the kind in the doorways of the Lausanne dress shops, during the summer, so that men could come at nightfall and take the girls they had caught during the day, choosing the heavi-

est and most golden, like nuggets in the gravel at
the bottom of the sluice-gates. She knew she was
thinking nonsense, but still, if she were a man, she
knew for certain she would like to find Juliette
struggling in the trap, then seize her in a wide-
meshed net, and torment such a prize at will. Juliette would have provided the instruction she lacked.

The pools between the tufts of dry reeds swarmed
with minnows that would be able to reach the sound
again at high tide. "Do you remember the little
sole?" Juliette asked.

Yes, she remembered. She had caught a little sole
in one of these pools, the day after they had come
to Santa Lucia, and she had held it for a long time
in the hollow of her hand, watching the little creature's rough back and then its mother-of-pearl belly
as it struggled, clapping against her palm with the
sound of a leaf shaken by the wind; so small that
it was almost transparent in the sun, the veins showing pink beneath the skin. Vanina had put it back
in the water at last, fascinated by the way it swam
that made it waver like a piece of sodden paper.
There was a strange correspondence between this
recollection and her preceding thoughts, and she
was amazed that Juliette's question had managed
to create it so deftly. It was not the first time she

had noticed how in requital (or recompense) for her defect of heaviness, her friend had received the gift of intuition.

Their footsteps on the shore of the sound had disturbed a whole world of sea life, invisible except for the river crabs whose eyes followed them as they slowly sank to the bottom of the tide pools, and ripples of violent eddies rushed to the surface as the creatures left the shallows. Swamp birds flew off at their approach, disappearing among the reeds. The still water had a vague odor of stagnation here, where no currents disturbed it, and spots of green and yellow mold, flashing in and out of the sunlight, provided a sumptuous decor for the maneuvers of water-striders, sea-scorpions, back-swimmers, and painted boatmen. Frogs fell like heavy fruits, keeping a critical distance, it appeared, as the two girls advanced. Their feet sank a little into a soft, lead-gray, nearly black soil where strangely shaped roots (those of the reeds were rather disturbing on account of their capricious anthropomorphism) and driftwood evenly covered with an admirable patina the color of anthracite were piled together like an archaeologist's trophies. There were the makings of a remarkable museum here, on the sole condition that the collector lean down and pick them up!

They did not take the trouble, for in this place
of stagnant water and blackened debris they found
the atmosphere immediately depressing, and Vanina decided that men of ancient times would have
chosen it for the habitation of a disagreeable god.
It was already the site of a colony of mosquitoes, at
least, whose bites forbode a fever. The girls felt a
sudden chill, despite the heat of the sun.

With one accord, they moved away from the shore
of the sound. Despite the thistles and thorns that
grew more fiercely in this sandy soil than other
places, they ventured into an unfamiliar region of
dunes between the sound's tide pools and the sea.
As low as they seemed from the beach, these dunes
held unsuspected hollows, and their little hillocks
enclosed sandy valleys where a man was completely
hidden as soon as he was no longer standing. The
girls sat down in one such gulley, in the sunlight, and
the heat was reflected upon them as if they were
before a garden wall. Juliette lighted a cigarette; and
rolled down into the sand, squirming like an animal
to show her pleasure. "It's good here," she said. "I'm
glad we came to Sardinia."

Everywhere on the slopes and summits of the
dunes grew sea lilies in clumps of white flowers and
long, bright green leaves, the only plant to flourish

so luxuriantly on the poor sustenance of a sand im-
pregnated with salt and clogged with shells and
other tidal debris. Their trumpets hung in clusters
at the tips of fleshy stems, and from them rose a
perfume that was extraordinarily powerful, fresh
even as it was heavy, acid and sweetish, insinuating,
combining the high tone sounded by the spring narcissus and the lower note of the autumn amaryllis,
capable of suffocating, like those bouquets it is wise
to take out of the bedroom at night. The heat inten-
sified their fragrance still further as it swept down
the sandy slope, spreading over them like a liquid.
Its influence was more toward nonchalance than
meditation, instilling the desire to do nothing but
lie still, saying nothing, watching the late-afternoon
moths that came to plunge their inordinate tongues
into each corolla. Sometimes a bird passed, hunting
insects on the wing. The daylight grew slightly
pink; the shadows lengthened, paled. But the girls
did not think of the time, since nothing urgent—
neither family nor school—awaited them at the
village, and they were free to let their intoxication
last the whole evening, if they chose.

When they stood up, the noises from the beach
had ceased long since, and the air gave them a sense
of coolness in contrast with the burning hollow

where they had been lying. Vanina threw over her
shoulders a great black shawl of soft and delicate
silk which she had taken from her room before
leaving, and draped a corner of it over Juliette as
well, so that she would be covered a little on their
way back. Their arms about one another's waists,
the girls crossed the dunes, taking the shortest way
back to the beach. Everywhere, on the low slopes
they slipped between, along the zigzagging path
all the way down to the water, or almost, bloomed
the same lilies. Juliette loved bouquets as only the
Swiss can (whose laws must be enforced by the
police to protect the flowers of the Alps), and she
did not resist the temptation to pick them; Vanina
followed her example; it was a sheaf of flowers that
they carried home between them, astonished, then
delighted to discover that the aromatic blooms, if
their calyxes were licked or bitten, tasted of the salt
they probably distilled from the far-flung spray on
stormy days.

They walked at the sea's edge when the sun disappeared. The moon would not appear for several
hours. They were alone before the calm water,
against the streaming light that rapidly lowered and
dimmed, disappearing from the upper skies. One
cloud floated above them, spread out like a great

jellyfish, pink still on its underside, against the encroaching green of the immensity, soon merely a shadow; several stars shone palely. There was light enough, and would be, to guide them on a path where every turning was familiar.

Juliette began to talk about the northern lights, tiresomely enough. Vanina listened absently, without taking part in the discussion, though she was much more learned than her friend and could have taught her as many things about the beautiful meteors that terrify nations when they come to fill the northern sky with fire and blood as about love and the burning aureole with which it crowns the women who have chosen to be wounded by it. But it was the latter point that her thoughts turned to, and she had promised herself not to breathe a word of them to a girl who would always be an innocent, despite her past (and her future, most assuredly) of ingenuous little obscenities.

Near the village, children ran out to stare at the foreigners, the "American queens," as the girls were called. In truth they cloaked themselves in a kind of royal mantle, which was the aroma of the sea lilies that protected them a little from the stench rising from the ground they were walking over, where all the villagers, or almost all, went at night-

fall to relieve themselves. The fishermen had returned long before, and had taken scarcely any
lobsters. In the house, Francesco, exhausted, was
already asleep; his wife greeted the girls sulkily;
the child was crying; there would be no conversation, no stories of souls, of serpents and eels, on the
doorstep tonight.

They went into their separate rooms, more to be
alone and quiet for a moment, to lie down and pass
the time, than to change their clothes (for what?).
Then it was time for the evening meal, which at
Santa Lucia di Siniscola they took very tardily, in
accordance with Vanina's wish and contrary to Juliette's: it was almost ten when they reached the
canteen that served as a restaurant, café, even
dance-hall, and they were not served at once, as
Juliette would have preferred, for there were many
people at the tables—some drinkers or merely on-
lookers rather than customers of consequence; the
waiter unceremoniously made several of them clear
out in order to give the girls a table to themselves
on the veranda facing the sea. This man (who was
the owner of the place as well, and a former sailor)
left as soon as he had seated them. It was a long
wait before he returned and offered them something
to eat; then there was a still longer wait until the

fish soup they had ordered was set before them.
Juliette had eaten up all the bread in her impatience.
The fish, however, were so varied and savory, there
was so much lobster and lobster-coral in a broth so
hot and so fragrant, the Malvoisian wine was so dry,
that even Juliette's bad humor did not resist it, for
she was gluttonous as a partridge, this innocent so
prodigal with her body, and it was again her opinion, after she had gobbled up what remained of
Vanina's portion as well as her own, that she was
"really glad to be in Sardinia." Vanina, who was
eating lightly, said that she was glad too, or to be
more exact, she was happy here.

They did not order fruit, suspicious of the water
it had been washed in, and asked only for very hot,
strong coffee. It was brought to them as black as
octopus ink, bitter despite the sugar, in little porce-
lain cups as thick in proportion to their size as the
walls of a dungeon. This time Juliette left half her
cup for Vanina, who took a third besides. She had
apparently decided not to close her eyes all night.

Flying insects crashed against the bulbs overhead;
they swirled, dazed, then fell and floundered on the
white paper tablecloth. There were mosquitoes and
gnats, tiny moths, and parasitical pine-beetles. Even

drinking fast, there were always a few tiny creatures
at the bottom of the glass or the cup.

The canteen had three or four rooms; it was
crudely built of whitewashed wood and corrugated
iron, with a wide veranda to shade it at noon. On
the wall near the kitchen window was fastened the
loudspeaker of a phonograph, and after the arrival
of the first customers on the terrace it blared the
same dance tunes and scratchy songs over and over
again. A few couples had formed at the start of the
evening and were revolving as well as they could
between the tables, bumping into chairs, getting in
the way of the busy waiters. People watched them
from outside, where the curious had formed several
rows, as if around a traveling show.

Later there were bravos, shouts: these were in
honor of the owner's friend, also a former sailor,
who came in with his accordion. The phonograph
was turned off, the tables were pushed toward the
walls in order to clear a space in the center. At the
first tango Juliette was asked to dance by a doctor
or pharmacist from Cagliari, a small brown hairy
man who had noticed the girls on the beach and at
each encounter offered to take them riding in his
car. Vanina declined one young man's invitation to

dance, and then another's, without having bothered to look at either. She did not greatly enjoy dancing, and decided she no longer had the right to put herself in another man's arms, and still less to let her body be touched, since she had chosen to give herself without reserve or condition to a lover who would bind her on the night that followed this, and would see her very soon. The moment, in fact, was not far off. She must not be inexact, she must be ahead of time at their first meeting in order to inaugurate worthily her status as a lover. She stood up. When Juliette returned to their table, Vanina was waiting for her standing up, and told her, without allowing her to sit down, that she was tired and wanted to go home right away. They would rest tomorrow, they would have dinner earlier and eat less heavily, and Juliette could dance as long as she liked.

Juliette was still laughing at her partner's jokes. She would have been glad to stay on alone, or at the doctor's table (for that was how he had introduced himself, emphatically), and the man would have asked for nothing better, but coming home she had to cross the room where the fisherman and his wife were sleeping, and she was afraid of disturbing them by coming in after Vanina. As for the window,

Juliette was far from imagining all the uses it might afford.

They left the restaurant, and in front of their house kissed each other and said good night.

Vanina was in her own room. She lit one candle, for there was no electricity in Francesco's house, and placed the stone against the door after having shut it, then attaching the string that secured it by two nails. This fragile barrier was more symbolic than effective, but Juliette did not linger before going to bed, and always fell asleep at once. Besides, she was a heavy sleeper.

The room was very small, very poor, but very clean, as is often the case in the houses of seafaring people. The walls were painted pale blue (intended to offend the flies!), beneath limed branches that supported the roof of reeds and leaves. The floor was of beaten earth, covered with a threadbare carpet. On one side was a commode of dark wood, half broken without being old, handles missing, and above it a set of shelves; then came a chair, though no table; on the other side was an iron bed with an insubstantial mattress laid across a webbing, a hard pillow, and an immense sheet (from the conjugal bed) folded in half. In one corner was a white enamel basin on an iron stand with a pail beneath

it, and a little mirror on the wall above. There was
also a wardrobe, behind a curtain, near the single
window. Some crabshells (of the species known as
"spider-crabs," which the fisherman and his wife
called "sea goats"), conches, pieces of mother-of-
pearl, and corals delicate as feathers were hung
around the set of shelves, alternating with pious
images and a colored print of Santa Rosalia. Vanina
had removed only some empty bottles from the
commode in order to replace them with various
toilet articles she had taken from her suitcases:
brushes of pale tortoise-shell, combs, gilt boxes,
flasks with silver stoppers, tweezers, tiny scissors,
and a fine hand-mirror. In the minds of Francesco
and Angela, all these were as precious as relics, and
they guarded them jealously, keeping their little
girl from touching them, and, above all, making
sure the neighbors did not know of their existence,
for there were lobster thieves who would rob even
their own relatives' nets, and who were certainly
capable of pilfering from a stranger.

Vanina had come to love this poor room, as you
might grow attached to a simple person or a pet that
once was wild. By having brought a little luxury
here, she felt as if she had embellished the desert,
and sometimes spilled two or three drops of perfume

on the floor by way of an offering. But on this night
she had something better than the pathetic chemis-
try of Parisian *haute couture*; she had the sea lilies
picked on the dunes; she had taken them from Juliette's hands as they were saying good night. The
great bouquet was lying on the chair. Vanina broke
off the stems that were too long, threw away the
pieces, and arranged the fragrant flowers in a wicker
basket between the bed and the window. There
could be no question of putting them in water, of
course, but flowers that had grown in salt and the
dry earth must be quite capable of enduring thirst
and drought.

Then she undressed completely, washed her feet
and wiped her body clean of the tiniest grains of
sand. Before she took off her wrist watch, she noticed it was almost eleven. There was not a minute
to lose. Nevertheless she loosened her hair and
combed it out very deliberately, finding it so dry
she could hear the crackling of the little sparks that
flowed beneath the tortoise-shell teeth with a blue
gleam, between the nape of her neck and her shoulders, while her hair puffed about her like a Persian
cat's fur. "I must be nervous to have so much electricity in me," she thought, lowering her mirror. It
was summer, of course, and she had always given

off sparks beneath the comb on nights of great heat.

She painted her lips a pale red, she brushed a little rouge into her cheeks with a tiny swansdown puff, then a little powder, she passed a sepia pencil over her lashes and along the edges of her eyelids, and even, for the points of her breasts were barely visible, had a sudden desire to darken them slightly with the eyebrow pencil. Upon reflection, however, she did nothing of the kind.

When she looked at herself in the mirror again, she decided she was pretty, and that a man would have to be irremediably foolish not to desire her. But it was growing late. She put the candle on the top shelf, lit another one beside it, and lay down on her bed. Juliette must have done the same (without so many preparations) some time ago, and was doubtless asleep, for nothing could be heard in the other room except a sound of regular breathing.

The candles burned with vertical flames, opposite the bed, spreading over it the gentlest light that could be desired. Between them was a little pink and blue plaster Madonna, its colors reminiscent of Near Eastern terra cottas. "Isis and the child Horus," Vanina thought, contemplating it affectionately, as if she had just discovered it at the bottom of a tomb.

And this time she did not wonder if the young man would come, for in some obscure fashion she was certain that nothing could keep him away.

She waited perhaps a quarter of an hour, preserving so perfect an immobility that her body seemed to have ebbed away, though her mind was wandering with the speed of lightning, and then, without her having heard the slightest noise from outside, she saw the shutter slowly opening. The young man was there, looking at her where she lay. "Above all, I hope he doesn't say anything," she thought, and she put a finger to her lips as she looked back at him, smiling no more than he. This slight movement was enough to call her back to consciousness and possession of her body, which had not ceased to be the subject of her reveries, but as an image, an object alien to her own person. She lay still for a brief moment more, until her heart was calmer, then let slip to the floor the half of the sheet that was covering her.

Then Vanina Mari was stark naked beneath the eyes of the man she had chosen to love. Naked save only for a necklace, a string of gold beads of ancient Genovese workmanship, which gleamed in the candlelight and accentuated the resemblance of the

young body to that of a little Egyptian dancer
carved in wood or ivory and set with precious stones.
She held her breath to show herself to him in the
most extreme abandon, like an inanimate object she
was inviting him to take, and because she had
stopped breathing her heart ceased for an instant,
then beat all the more wildly. Her breasts were very
round and pure in outline, small moreover, superbly
distended; her waist was long and slender above
hips that were a little full though not heavy, and her
legs were very thin, with long, perfectly rounded
thighs. From emotion or exposure to the sun, her
skin had taken a pinkish cast that was almost brilliant in the warm light that fell from the candles;
her fleece was very dark and glossy, curly too, vigor-
ous and violent. While she showed herself, Vanina
thought of what the young man was seeing from
the window, and imagined she was looking for the
first time at her own body, thrown on a miserable
bed in a Sardinian fisherman's cottage. She thought,
too, that she was lying in a state of complete nudity
in front of a window opening onto the great, wild
night, and that there was the cold and restless sea
behind the man who soon would be her lover. These
thoughts filled her with undreamed of pleasure: it

was as if she had never known herself before, and had at last discovered her soul at the same time she perceived the forms of her body. She told herself she was "exposed" (which was certainly the truth); she was proud of having been imprudent and bold enough to dare such a mad exposition. A prop and stimulus to her enthusiasm, the fragrance of the lilies had filled the room, and it undulated in the air about her like a cloud of incense, so heavy it could almost be caressed or cut with a knife. Between the white flowers and the black hair, so close to each other, a somewhat mysterious harmony had been established, strengthened by the body's nakedness. Vanina was lying stark naked in her loosened hair and in the odor of the sea lilies. The young man was looking at her by candlelight.

Such was the scene for a long moment. They could hear the sound of the waves. Suddenly, perhaps from his movement to grasp the sill, or else from his expression, Vanina knew that the man could no longer remain merely a spectator, and was about to leap into the room.

"No," she said (in a whisper, so that Juliette could not hear her if she happened to be awake). "Tomorrow. . . . Go away now."

Regretfully, the young man obeyed. Vanina remained as she was for several minutes more, then
stood up. The darkness outside the window was
empty. She closed the shutters, latching them this
time, before lying down again.

She did not sleep at all that night, in accordance with the plan she had made, or almost not at all, for she was thinking of what was going to happen to her on the next night. It was hot, and her body perspired, and the bed was too narrow for her to find a cool place on it by turning over. Nevertheless she remained covered, for it was to expose herself that she had lifted the sheet, and now that the young man was gone she believed it was her duty to him not to remain naked in the solitude and the darkness. All the coffee she had drunk made her heart flutter. She would have drunk even more to make it beat still more wildly. Sudden images occurred to her, flashing through her mind like the discharge of an electric potential. Her eyes fixed on the face she imagined to be inclined toward her own, she saw it wheeling across the sky, whirling as it closed in upon her like a kind of celestial Sicily, like a constellation that had strayed below the moon and the other stars. This spiraling movement gave her the sense that she was to be pulverized by it, pinioned to the ground, and then, comet or countenance, it filled the whole sky and faded away into the night. Then she gave way to an infinite beatitude which was this night itself, and which was her lover's face turned to night, beneath a dispersion of luminous points.

"Truly," she said to herself, "he is already my lover, since tomorrow I shall be surrendered to him. He is the master of my body and my being." Ten times, twenty, a hundred or still more, her imagination recomposed the features of the man she called her lover and her master, though they vanished as fast as she summoned them into being. Yet that he should dissolve into an incandescent shower, like fireworks, was not displeasing to her fantasy. Her lips formed the word "glory," which is the name of the pyrotechnic device for producing this marvelous effect, and still half open, sought for a kiss; her nostrils breathed in the scent of the lilies.

It was wonderful with what fidelity she found again the slightest details of the face the window had framed while she was exhibiting herself to the young man. She recalled perfectly the dark brilliance of his eyes, his black and bushy brows, his rather large ears, the fine curve of his nose and the handsome contour of his mouth, his perfect teeth. Yet she recovered with difficulty or not at all the sound of his voice as she had heard it in the pine grove. Was it not her own fault? She had almost not let him speak at all, had even kept him from telling her his name.

She wondered if he would remember with as

much exactitude what she had had the audacity to show him. Had she succeeded in engraving on the young man's memory, and indelibly, the image of her naked body? Gleaming in the light of her two candles, laid out like a lifeless object, she had submitted to his gaze for a long time. "It is curious," she said to herself, "that for me he is above all a face, and that I want to be a body for him. . . . That must be the way it is, in love."

Where did he live? She had no idea, preferring to forego the domestic details in the background of the still somewhat ideal character she had conceived such passion for. She was entirely indifferent to what he might be doing at this very moment; whether he had gone home as soon as he had seen her; whether he was wandering off into the night—along the shore, at the edge of the pine grove, across the dunes—like a drunkard or a madman; whether he was asleep or dreaming, and if dreaming, whether his dreams were of her, or if he could not sleep, whether his thoughts were drifting toward what the girl's promises held in store for him. Only one thing preoccupied her, which was to be sure of giving him, the next night, every possible pleasure, and not to disappoint him—not only in what he expected of her (she took no heed of that, she wanted to give much

more), but in what she herself expected from a girl
in love. Of course she would have to think about it,
make good use of her time. The whole night was not
too long for preparing the event, arranging it like a
royal wedlock (in other words: like a mechanical
ballet).

She was pleased to discover that not only the
great heat, but the skimpy mattress and the lumps in
the bed helped her stay awake. Several questions
occurred to her. What to wear was more urgent than
the rest. Yes. How was she to dress appropriately for
such an occasion as the surrender of her body to an
almost unknown young man on the deserted beach?
It was impossible to come to meet him naked, for
she did not wish to seem shameless, and besides,
the carabiniers might apprehend her on their rounds
and do her some violence.

Black seemed suited to the ceremonial of submission. Dissolving into the darkness, it would help her
to pass unseen, if someone happened to be spying
on her at the time of the assignation. Then too it
somehow consecrated her to the nocturnal powers
a lover incarnated, as she vaguely realized in her
inmost heart, and it signified that having silenced
her judgment and her will, annulled all spirit of

independence, she now was delivering herself body and soul to the world of darkness.

Hence in spite of a certain reluctance she discarded the red linen shorts she had decided on at first, and chose instead a rather long black skirt of light silk, with a sleeveless, V-necked blouse of the same color and cloth. She thought that he would be pleased to find her shoulders bare when he opened the blouse, and that straps looked stupid and ugly. Of course, she could have omitted a brassiere altogether, for her breasts, without being too light, were not such that they needed support in order to bear themselves proudly; but on reflection she decided on a strapless brassiere that fastened in back like a tiny black corset. She had hesitated to pack it for the trip, doubting that she would ever have any use for it in this poor country, and now she rejoiced at having done so, since it seemed made for just such an occasion, and nothing could have been more seemly beneath a young captive's sheer blouse. Perfectly familiar with her wardrobe, she searched her memory as she might have ransacked her suitcases had they been open before her, weighing, choosing, and rejecting each article with an attention so concentrated that without moving a finger beneath the sheet she could virtually feel the crumpling of the stuffs, the sleek softness of the leathers.

No jewelry (despite the Polynesian girls' example). Neither necklace nor rings nor earrings (let him see the tiny holes in her lobes for wearing antique loops). The rule of humility forbidding any exception in sumptuary matters, the only tolerable ornament would be, perhaps, a flower. Even the wrist watch would remain in the cottage, on the shelf between the candles, opposite the bed. Since she had resolved to love a man and, even if it should be for a single night, to yield herself into his hands without the slightest restriction, she had no right to dispose of time, no power to measure on a dial attached to her wrist the hours and minutes engulfed in sacrifice and servitude.

As for the mechanics of love, its concrete operation, or, in vulgar terms, the encounter of flesh with flesh, she had read during the last year at school in Lausanne Forberg's *Erotology*, *The Dialogues of Luisa Sigea* (in Latin), Sade's *Philosophy in the Boudoir*, and *The Confessor's Manual*, which is to say that she knew everything her body was capable of. Yet she had always declined, in the coldest and most discouraging manner, the merest kiss or improper caress, whether boy's or girl's, though her less erudite companions rarely denied one another such things, not to mention their sequel. It was enough for her to know, and now she rejoiced at having learned and kept her knowledge to herself, for had she acted differently the gift to her beloved would not have been so rare as she would have it. Utterly available, yes, that was how she would be at the moment of surrender, and the fact that she would be intact enhanced such availability, but still required the knowledge of every practice, every violence, every possible excess, in order for the submission to assume its ultimate worth and be something beyond that of an idiot girl who has been seduced, or of an animal that has been tamed. Feverishly she began testing her memory, anxious not to have forgotten any of those pages secretly devoured behind a rampart of grammars and lexicons. Already the sun was high, and the shutter, fitting imperfectly against the window, let a wide beam of light into the room before she had finished reviewing her lessons.

Later on, she decided that her scholarship, even if it had several gaps, was certainly more extensive than the young man's experience, and that she would acquit herself honorably. And her mind's tension slackened as her anxiety evaporated. A great weariness followed, overcoming her entirely; sleep broke over her like a wave rolling clumps of seaweed in its wake, and she lost consciousness, while shouts and laughter outside the window testified to the life which daylight had restored to the village.

She would have slept soundly despite them, but Juliette had been awake for some time, disturbed by the fisherman's wife at work in the next room and by the child in tears and brawling. After putting the water over the charcoal fire to boil between the andirons of the hearth, Juliette untied the latchstring, pushed the stone aside, and walked into Vanina's room. She exclaimed aloud several times and shook the yawning girl in her bed.

"What a smell!" she cried, pointing to the basket of lilies. "You might have died from asphyxiation. You pretend to be so serious and so wise, but you're crazier than any girl I know. Yes, crazy to keep a bouquet like that in your bedroom without even opening the shutters. No wonder you can't wake up. Don't you have a headache? Come drink some tea, it will do you good.

"Oh," she continued, "I didn't know you slept raw now. So do I . . . in all this heat, it's cooler: if there weren't so many flies I'd have done without the sheet too."

Vanina did not have a headache, but she felt
rather hungry, and she always wanted tea when
someone offered it to her. Leaving the shutters to
her friend, she indolently climbed out of bed and
slipped on a hooded dressing gown that was almost
a legend in Lausanne, where her friends at school
called it Pope Joan's robe because it was made of
white silk with long golden embroideries and a
purple sash. Her disordered hair, her bare feet, her
eyes that a sleepless night had dilated until they
looked as if she had taken belladonna, gave her a
strange beauty that was a little out of place by daylight. Juliette was not so blind as to see nothing of
this, but held her tongue, deciding that if her beautiful friend looked a little "out of this world," the
poisonous lilies were to blame; she was far from
imagining the cruel country Vanina was abandoning
now, and from which she would painfully return,
after traveling there in earnest, tomorrow at dawn.

In Juliette's room they ate toasted slices of black
bread dipped in honey. The tea tasted strongly of
smoke, which they affected to consider "Chinese,"
but which was almost unendurable.

Juliette lighted the day's first cigarette. Vanina
handed her a shell ashtray (a "Venus" clam) so she
would not burn the sheet and sat down at the win-

dow. A scruple had awakened or rather revived her
nightlong anxiety that she might seem clumsy or silly
because of her inexperience, when the young man
would seize her—might behave awkwardly and later
regret it, when she would know better than theoreti-
cally her *métier* as a lover. She had an idea she
rejected at first but which on reflection seemed a
good one. When the cigarette was finished she asked
Juliette to come with her into the other room, which
was the farthest from the Carones, because she
wanted to tell her something in secret, without being
overheard by Angela or the child.

There, she attached the string that served as a
latch and knotted it carefully, shoved the stone
back in place, and closed the shutter once more.
Juliette, sitting on the disordered bed, laughed at
her and asked if she intended to asphyxiate them
both, if that was the promised "secret." Her slippers
had fallen off her feet, and her robe, its belt missing, gaped a little. She was very surprised when
Vanina sat down next to her, put one arm around
her neck, and entreated her quite seriously to teach
her then and there everything she had learned about
kissing from either boys or girls. At first Juliette
protested, wanting to joke some more. With no suc-
cess. Vanina was to be obeyed, her every require-

ment satisfied. What followed was no revelation for the latter, who intended only to take advantage of a practice session, but Juliette, who had originally regarded their experiments as a joke, soon found herself taking them quite seriously and did not long conceal the nature of her excitement, nor the pleasure she was feeling. When she moaned rather sharply, Vanina thought, "I am giving pleasure," and was not altogether content to have given Juliette what she wished only the young man to enjoy. Nevertheless she was flattered, as if she had received a qualifications certificate from a difficult examining board, her anxiety had vanished, since it was obvious she did not lack skill. Nevertheless, the moan had shocked her. She determined not to imitate Juliette in that, to hold her breath if need be, and to observe the rule of silence, as she had been accustomed to do, as a little girl, whenever the nuns would punish her.

The girls continued their sport (or their study), one to inform herself more thoroughly, the other because she never had enough of what she enjoyed. Time passed; they paid no attention. They went to the beach, that day, much later than usual.

As they left the house, Angela, who was playing with the child on the doorstep, told them the east

wind had risen and the sea would be rough: they
would do better to go for a walk under the pines
today. The boats had left during the night, when
the sea was still calm, to collect the lobster pots
dropped the day before, but there would almost
certainly be no lobsters, and even the pots might
be lost. To make matters worse, the wind made the
little girl nervous; she was crying and petulantly
tossing pebbles at Vanina's mousekin. It would take
gumdrops to keep her still. Good. Gumdrops were
purchased for the sake of the mousekin, then the
girls had walked down to the beach. There was in
fact a slight wind from the open sea, and a few
waves, though hardly very terrifying ones, rolled
bunches of seaweed up the beach, yet there was
nothing troublesome enough in such manifestations
to explain the bathers' prudence: of those who came
daily for the sun and the sea, most were absent now.
The mountain people had made off, probably at
dawn, and there was nothing to be seen but some
garbage and the ruts where they had camped in
their cart. A few children were running after a tall
girl in a wet shift. An old man was walking alone
toward the fisheries, picking up driftwood and pieces
of cork with a long spiked staff, tossing them in a
sack he carried over one shoulder.

The handsome young man, of course, was no longer a part of the picture. Vanina, after a quick look up and down the beach as far as she could see, was relieved to find there was nothing on the sand that could remind her of the familiar silhouette. Nothing resembling it in the water either. She would have been quite disappointed had he not understood that it was his duty not to reappear before nightfall.

They plunged into the water, which was not cold, yet they did not go so far out as on the other days. Little clouds passing in front of the sun obscured it for moments at a time, and then the girls felt they were not so strong or so courageous. The waves slapped at them incessantly, making it hard to breathe. Soon back on the beach, Vanina wanted to show Juliette the game she had invented with the tiger beetles, but the wind must have impeded the short flights of these insects or blown them into the dunes, for like the gnats that were their habitual prey, the tiny carnivores were not in evidence. On the other hand there were clouds of sand fleas near the stranded seaweed.

"The weather's going to change," Juliette remarked.

These were the first words, or almost the first, she had spoken since they had been in the water.

She leaned over her friend's face where Vanina lay stretched out on her back, and her voice had a gentle intonation not usually within its range, an inflection that betrayed how near she had been to saying something else. If she had a particular notion of "change" in her head, it was certainly not a question of wind or calm, of dry or rainy weather.

"Oh," Vanina said, "I don't think so. The wind will clear the sky, and it will be beautiful tonight."

Vanina's accents also lacked a certain frankness, the determining element of her sentence being "tonight," around which the words had organized themselves without her paying too much attention to their arrangement. It was apparent that for both girls, without their having made any concerted effort, the capital (or crucial) word had been the last one spoken. Had they any suspicion of this, some evidence of their mutual mistrust? They looked into each other's eyes. Such a conversation would have continued uncomfortably, even awkwardly in reserve and desultoriness. Juliette decided to fling herself down on the sand beside Vanina, her head lying on a corner of the beach robe that happened to be free. Their hair lying loose and mingled, keeping their thoughts to themselves, both girls gave themselves up to the sun, though it burned through

the clouds only intermittently and shadows came
often enough to rouse them from their stupor.

They returned to the village much later than
usual. The restaurant was almost empty when they
sat down for lunch, the waiter had disappeared, and
they had to call and call before they were served
what was left of the day's lobsters. With the help of
bread, muscat grapes (washed or not, they would
take their chances), and strong wine, they made a
lunch out of it, but there was no coffee to be had,
for the pressure was not high enough in the steam
boiler. Back at the cottage, each girl went to her
own room. Vanina fell on her bed fully (though
lightly) dressed, for she had sleep to make up before
nightfall.

After a long afternoon nap, Juliette had called
her friend several times. Receiving no sign of life
from the sleeper, and not wanting to force the door
behind which, more than absence or insensibility,
she feared to meet with a hostile reception, she had
joined Angela, who was knitting on the doorstep
while the child rolled in the dust with her play-
mates, squabbling over an old horseshoe. Soon there
was a circle of chairs beside their own, a ring of old
women and young mothers, brides and girls—the
fishermen's wives, who asked the foreign girl questions about her country. Since Juliette had difficulty
understanding what was being said to her, she generally answered incorrectly, which was of little im-
portance, moreover, for the women understood her
no better. To amuse herself she was stuffing the child
with gumdrops like a Strasbourg goose; the little
girl was so greedy that two bags disappeared one
after the other without satiating her, and a tantrum
threatened each time another child was offered a
share in the treat. Had Vanina come back (if she
had gone for a walk), awakened (if she had been
asleep), or cheered up (in the third hypothesis)?
Juliette called her again, to make sure, from time
to time, but not too loudly, for she suspected her
friend was in one of her moods.

In fact the girl heard her perfectly well, but had no desire to make an appearance before dinnertime, and remained lying where she was in her half-darkened room. A fantasy ensnared (or enslaved) her, its origin a ray of sunlight from a crack in the shutter, at the moment when the sun had reached the horizon and cast a red spot in front of her, changed to purple the blue-painted wall. Before disappearing, the spot had swelled, assuming the curiously distinct form of a feline paw surmounted by the muzzle and mane of a lion, and at this moment Vanina had imagined a great red lion encountered in the dunes, at twilight on the almost violet sands. It was like this: the lion rested his claws on the belly of a naked girl to mark her, it seemed, with his seal, after which she disappeared into a hollow of the ground while another girl succeeded her and lay down at full length on the sand with a sort of happiness, and another girl waited behind this second one to take her place when it was empty, and still others behind her, and at the sea's edge a line of these creatures as far as the sharpest eye could reach. All had their hands tied behind their backs with heavy, well-knotted cords, and yet, their necks swaying gently, they walked toward the beast with exultant mien. Their heads and bodies had been completely shaved; they no longer had eyebrows or even lashes, which in some inexplicable way made Vanina identify them with the moon and oppose them to the sun. "To take one's place among women branded by the sun," Vanina thought, "is the role of virgins, followers of the moon. It will be my role this very night. Perhaps my surrender will be displayed to better advantage if I shave my hair—no, I will do no such thing, for it would be a deception not to give myself to the man just as I showed myself to him yesterday, and I think it might provide him less pleasure if I offered him my belly smooth as an almond, my head shaved like a young convict's." At certain moments in the daydream she confused the man soon to be her lover with the lion, substituted him for the red beast. Then the lion grew dominant again. He was amazingly hairy (in compensation for the razor?) and his mane had a strange, almost chemical luster, burning with neither flame nor smoke above the white bodies of the prostrate girls.

With her daydream mingled a recollection from her childhood, the memory of a red-haired farmer with a heavy beard, great mustaches, and a tremendous growth of hair all over his body, of which the (imaginary) beast had doubtless inherited some-

thing. This farmer, who was called Giacomo, had
been the cheesemaker on one of Count Mari's es-
tates somewhere between Lodi and Bergamo. A
close though not quite innocent friendship had developed between him and Vanina during a summer
she had spent at the villa adjoining the farm, when
she was almost eight years old. Each time she deceived her nurse's vigilance (an easy matter, for the
war, still in the early stages, had distracted the woman's attention from her task), the little girl would
run to the cheese shed where Giacomo was the sole
authority, feigning insanity to avoid military service,
sullen with any adult, insolent to the bailiff, peevish
with Count Mari and his brother, who dealt gently
with him so that he would stay on, for this churlish
man knew cheese the way only a handful of scholars
know Greek and Latin, the way a virtuoso knows
the violin. No one would have come to look for
Vanina in the dim old shed (formerly a carriage-
house), where Giacomo would pick her up under
the arms, set her down in front of him on one of
the many ladders, and let her taste the fresh cheese
that was overflowing the heavy molds as thick as
cartwheels, stacked on ten or twelve shelves of massive planks around the walls. Giacomo's great hand
plunged into a vat, while Vanina was gorging her-

self, and began rubbing her legs, then her thighs
with a mixture of cream cheese and whey. Soon he
had taken off her shoes and underthings, and thrusting his hand under her dress (which was light and
loose because of the heat), rubbed her whole body
up to her chin with the soft white liquid. He told
her she would have a smooth skin all over when she
was grown up; the *contesse*, he said, had used this
recipe for over a hundred years, and they had always
found it successful. Sometimes too, when he had
set the little girl high up on the ladder, he would
lick her feet, lick her thighs, her belly, snorting like a
horse, threatening that she tasted so good he would
eat her down to the bones. Vanina would laugh,
while he held her on the ladder and she felt his hard
beard against her. "Lion," she would tell him then
(she remembered it perfectly), "you will not eat me.
Let me go now, let me go or I'll call the hunters,
and they'll come with guns to kill you." But no one
came, and struggle as she would, he did not let her
go for a long time.

The bailiff's daughter, a certain Medea, who
showed more than her ten years, also came to the
cheese-shed that summer. She had told Vanina that
Giacomo would make her cover all his man's body
with whey, so that his skin would be smooth too.

She was, of course, only a bailiff's daughter, and Giacomo knew the world no less than cheeses. He never dared ask such a service from the *contessina*. Naturally, the two girls maintained an absolute silence about their relations with the cheesemaker and confided only in each other, proud to have a secret to share, and the grown-ups never found out about what was happening in the shed.

As her recollection of Giacomo faded, Vanina allowed the red lion to replace it, knowing that the image was inseparable from what she would undergo (wound and wonder) in a few hours' time. Thus the distant past prepared the way for the near future. Yet while her mind wandered with almost feverish agitation, she remained quite motionless, forcing herself to lie still, and neither touched nor caressed her body (as she habitually did when daydreaming), as if already it had ceased to belong to her.

The time slipped away. It was late. Night had fallen ouside, and Juliette was tired of calling. Vanina leaped off her bed, lit the two candles on the shelf, two more (three in one room were bad luck) near the washstand. She stripped herself naked and washed her feet again (with an obsessive concern for their cleanliness), washed her hands, her face,

and with a fresh towel carefully wiped her whole
body, though without washing it, for in the state
of abandon to which she had consented in advance,
she was willing to be still a trifle salty from the sea,
and she thought it would please the young man.
Naked still (for to dress, this time, seemed her last
move, like the last act before an execution, and
she wished to postpone it as long as possible), she
brushed and combed her hair for several minutes,
so it would be quite free of sand, as light and soft
on her shoulders as it had been the night she had
displayed herself—even lighter, even softer. At last
she put on her clothes, without varying from her
decisions of the night before. Nevertheless, and
purely by chance, the open suitcase offered her a
pair of red, almost magenta nylon panties that had
the brilliant luster of a peony petal. A "frivolity" of
American manufacture, she had bought them in
Switzerland and never worn them. She put them on
now, for the color was imperative, as well as a pair
of red velvet slippers, and no stockings.

In the next room Juliette was reading a week-old
paper by the light of a single candle, her eyes straining to make out the tiny letters in a language that
was not much more intelligible to her than the conversation of the women of Santa Lucia. She was

THE GIRL BENEATH THE LION 103

thinking she might just as well hold the newspaper upside down. "No," she said to Vanina, "no, I guess I'll never learn Italian. . . . Did you make yourself so pretty for dancing tonight? The boys won't be able to look at anyone else. Wait for me a minute, will you? I'm really too dirty, I'll change so we won't look like the princess and the beggarmaid. But why put on a silk dress and then no makeup? You must have powder and lipstick—I've seen you wear them, often. Do you want mine, if you don't feel like going back for yours?"

No, Vanina did not want powder, or lipstick either. She said so succinctly, without explaining (it was quite impossible to explain) that she must keep her face naked, and that even if she had used cosmetics the night before, lying beneath the man's gaze like a corpse in the candlelight, motionless, untouchable, remote, she would endure no mask, no manner of protective ornament at the moment she was to surrender herself into the same man's hands like an object consecrated to every contact and to every violence. Juliette was hesitating between skirts. Then, in the twinkling of an eye, she pulled on a beige angora sweater over her bare skin, and a pair of tight-fitting rust-colored trousers, both colors flattering to her complexion. She painted her

mouth wide with a bright orange lipstick, powdered
her face pale, and shook out her short hair. "There!"
she said. "I'm ready. I don't care if my sunburn
scratches, or if I leave wool all over my partners.
Now tell me, what do you think of me as a boy?"

She wanted her words to remind Vanina of what
had happened during the morning, when she had
followed her into the other room, and perhaps to
disconcert her as well. Without results, for the other
girl had already forgotten the experiment; she answered absently that Juliette looked very well that
way, and that it was time to go to dinner.

The wind had dropped, the air was warmer than
at noon. The idlers around the restaurant gave it the
look of a zoo at feeding-time, and the girls had to
elbow their way past old people and children, shov-
ing men aside to clear themselves passage to the
door. On such occasions Juliette worked miracles:
she had that easy good-hearted brutality not excep-
tional among northern peoples (conductors in Swiss
buses grasp your arm and "put you in your place"),
while for Vanina it was a struggle to touch another
person, unless she was angry. After having served
them several curses while they were passing, the
circle showered them with compliments that had
nothing modest about them, when they were on the

terrace; for the two "foreigners" were the stars of
the show, and their wardrobe beyond the spectators'
wildest dreams.

The menu was the customary one: fish, squid, lobster. The train had brought mussels from Olbia, but
no meat—the meat would come tomorrow, most
likely. Except for rice and spaghetti, tomatoes, egg-
plants, grapes—and except for a poacher's hare served
with great mystery so the sergeant of the carabiniers
would not suspect the cheat—the girls had eaten
nothing since they had come to Santa Lucia that
was not fish, mollusk, or crustacean. Vanina found
herself wondering if there was not something un-
healthy, even poisonous, in a continual seafood diet;
perhaps they would find themselves physically and
spiritually contaminated, if they had hitherto escaped, by having absorbed so much phosphorus, so
much iodine, so much salt at each of their meals.
There would be no more meat tomorrow than any
other day, of course. Besides, what difference did
it make what she was served tomorrow, since the
first issue she was destined for was love, and love
was to be met with tonight! Tomorrow was further
than Lausanne, than China! Perhaps there would be
no tomorrow. But now, right now, she would have
liked some meat.

She ate lightly, drank even less wine than usual, and even more coffee. Juliette was talkative, and Vanina found it pleasant to let her continue without interruption, nodding now and then so her friend would think she was listening, but hearing only noise. The accordionist had come, and begun with a Neapolitan tango; two men ("mainlanders," certainly) were singing, their voices straining against the instrument; the waiter pushed back the tables to make room, overturning bottles in his haste; one couple was dancing already.

Almost at once there were others on the narrow floor; a local girl was doing her best to please everyone, tall and quite pretty in her sailor's blouse, her dark blue trousers, and the little varnished boots she lost each time steps changed, showing her strong feet. Her hair was as short as a boy's and very black, her eyes black too, her skin burnt, her Saracen look well suited to her boldness. The men all wanted to dance with her, and she glanced proudly at the women as she passed in their arms.

Her victory came to an end, or was at least divided, when Juliette, after having eaten greedily, downed the rest of the wine on top of the coffee and accepted an invitation to dance, for from then on the men competed for the foreign girl, who did

not miss one dance. The Swiss girl being a little
taller than her Santa Lucia counterpart (who was not
wearing heels), both were much taller than the other
women dancing, and both were the only ones—as if
they had consulted each other beforehand—wearing
trousers and sweaters cut like a man's. In their
movements among the tables, on the arms of men
for the most part rather short, they looked like two
noble pieces hurled into battle among the pawns of
a dizzying chessboard. Two towers, the black and
the white, that literally dominated the dance. As
for Vanina, in accordance with her habitual con-
duct, she refused to dance each time she was asked,
despite the insistence of several young men who had
noticed her on the beach and would have been
proud to look like her intimates. The blood throbbed
in her temples from the excessive amount of coffee
she had drunk (from time to time she asked for another cup), and she smiled, imagining that the bitter
liquid whose fragrance rose from the burning porce-
lain mug was perhaps a brew of hemlock, belladonna, or henbane. Had she really thought it was,
she would probably have emptied the cup no less
eagerly. Juliette and the Santa Lucia girl approached
each other, moved away again, whirled about, but
she kept her eyes fixed on them, dazed but fasci-

nated. She moved her chair back a little when someone bumped into it, without saying a word. Her
will was fading, had almost disappeared, but the
only point on which she remained firm was not to
dance, not to let herself be taken in the arms of one
of these little men, since the arms of the one she
had chosen, the one she loved, were going to take
her soon.

She was alone at the table, though not in the
least bored, for Juliette had discovered it was easier
to remain standing than to be forever sitting down
and getting up again. The man with the accordion
passed the hat, played a last dance in gratitude,
then went away, and many couples left with him.
But others, persevering, wanted more music and
insisted that the phonograph be connected again.
Among the women only Juliette and the dark girl
remained, and five or six men argued over them for
a waltz, then a tango, always the same ones, that
the phonograph ground out; then the dark girl
dropped out and her last partner, a stranger in the
village, took her arm to leave with her in the direction of the pine grove. Then the phonograph was
turned off for good. Juliette took leave of her young
men and returned to the table, asking if Vanina was
annoyed with her at being abandoned. No, it would

not have occurred to Vanina to be annoyed, but the waiter had disappeared, the steam boiler was empty, there had been no fresh coffee for over an hour, everyone had gone home to sleep, and they would be the last to leave.

It is true enough that during the week, people go to bed early in Santa Lucia di Siniscola. On their way (a few steps), the girls met no one, saw no light behind the shutters. The dust was white beneath the moon. They slipped into the house without making any noise.

After having crossed the first room in darkness, in order not to waken the sleepers, they lighted the candles in the second, Juliette's room. Vanina said good night to her friend, kissed her, but when the other girl, grown heavy and limp, tried to go into the third room with her, it was no use, Vanina pushed her away, pretending not to understand her intention (which was to continue the morning's "experiments" in Vanina's bed), closed the door, shoved the stone into place, and knotted the string. What did it matter if Juliette was disappointed, if she had to go to bed alone? A creaking bed, then silence indicated that the big girl had quickly resigned herself to her fate.

The sea lilies in the basket, though they had not

had a single drop of water since they had been picked, were as fresh as the day before, and their fragrance was no less violent, no less suave. Vanina broke off a spray of the blossoms and fastened them to her blouse. She looked at her watch lying on the shelf. It was time. Leaving the shutter half-open, as she had done when she went to the pine grove, she jumped down from the window.

The moon already hung a little lower in the sky than when they had left the dance-hall, but its light was so intense that the night seemed fantastically extended, and in its illuminated solitude Vanina felt as insignificant as if she were in the desert, as if the limits of the world had been projected to infinity. The mountain danced before her eyes with no more stability than a vapor; the pines, showing no relief, only their dark color, were indistinguishable from the fields and the vines, the dunes from the reeds; the sea was as firm as a shining skin stretched across a drum the size of the universe. What a noise, if a palm commensurate had made it sound! A streak of sulfur flashed across this leather sea—the moon's reflection in the still water. No wind —not even a breath. Nothing, the girl thought, is so indescribable as a beautiful night.

She was walking slowly, cautiously (like a house cat venturing into wet grass), past the canteen and several wretched houses ranged in a row. The last building in the village, more of a lean-to than a house, rose a little ahead of her, on a low hillock beyond the beach where the stranded boats were sleeping. The path sloped down, then mounted again, strewn with pebbles and sharp cinders, splinters of glass and earthenware crockery, pieces of rusty iron, all kinds of garbage; it divided at the deserted house, and Vanina took the narrower section along the rocks that jutted out over the sea, for the moon showed it clearly, and she could see where she was putting her feet with less danger of injuring or dirtying herself. She wanted to avoid all risks, however slight, before having reached the goal she had determined on in order to expose herself to the greatest risks and suffer the hardest trials. Behind the building the sand from the dunes lay heaped against the walls and obstructed the door without any measures having been taken, it seemed, to keep it from coming back on windy days. Vanina had realized that this shadowy, uneven ground was a favorite place for the villagers to relieve themselves, and the sea lilies probably thrived on the manure replenished nightly, for here the white flowers showed exuberantly above the sand in which their leaves were three-quarters buried.

Then the path fell again. The night recovered its purity once she had passed the fecal zone. When Vanina reached the beach, its smooth sand stretching more than two miles before her, she stopped a moment, breathed deeply to feel the life within her move like the air in her lungs, the blood in her veins; she decided she had never been so marvelously wide

awake. Then, for she had suddenly decided to go
barefoot to her lover, she took off her pretty velvet
slippers and set them down near a stump that made
a good landmark, buried in the sand save for a long,
rough back and something like a skull, the shape of
a sleeping crocodile.

The feeling of going barefoot surprised her, for
she expected nothing so overwhelming: a sensation
neither pleasure nor pain, but instead a profound
disturbance from which the best or the worst might
develop. She realized that nakedness had laid its
hand upon her; she decided there must be at least
two categories of nakedness (not counting those per-
taining to the soul, which are innumerable), since
the one—and obviously her state when exposed to
her lover was of this first class—was forbidden at
the same time that it was provocative, a transparent
armor for the vulnerable young body, while the
second kind, suggested now by the act of walking
barefoot, was a capitulation, a voluntary rape, an
invitation to defilement. She turned around, after
having walked a few steps farther, to look again
at the old olive or oak stump worn by the waves,
bleached by the salt, split by the noonday heat into
a yawn spiked with toothlike splinters terrible in
the moonlight. It was to this monstrous guardian

she had entrusted the first piece (the key) of her armor, the others severed now, ready to fall at the slightest blow. She was scarcely conscious of the silk against her damp skin, so warmly did the night air caress her, so closely did the wet sand cling to her feet like mouths as she walked. By abandoning her shoes, she had renounced in advance every last-minute defense, had surrendered all freedom to dispose of her own body. She was delivered, wrists already bound, in accordance with the strange desire that had occurred to her and that (more strangely still) she had expressed to the violent young man who was perhaps watching her now, and who would soon be upon her.

Sometimes—was it so strange, after all— she forgot the face of this man she had promised herself to, and she imagined it was to all of nature that she surrendered herself by yielding to the violent hands of a man she had nevertheless sworn she "loved"; it seemed to her that in this coming embrace, on which she dwelt with fear and rapture, she would be dissolved into sea and sand and wind, would know the heat of elemental fires beyond its cold reflection in the moonlight. She was walking at the sea's edge especially to savor the moist contact, and

she noticed a little sucking sound beneath her feet
whenever she sank deeper into wetter sand.

Before her, as far as the eye could reach, bun-
dles of seaweed stranded by the afternoon squalls
stretched out along the shore like characters written
in obscure ink on an inordinate scroll, indecipher-
able combinations that, besides the letters of some
alphabet, might just as well have been the code of
love in Balinese, Tibetan, or Zuñi, in the places
where the tide had flung them together more abun-
dantly. Lights gleamed out to sea, then vanished: the
lighthouses of the Bay of Olbia, marking the reefs
with that electric wink that is a sign of pleasure in all
streets of ill fame. At the gulf's extremity, among
the pines and a few low houses, rose the little tower
of La Caletta, shaped like a huge cactus with a
single orange flower at its tip—another signal. And
Vanina, when she looked behind her, saw the high,
square tower crowned with battlements that marked
the site of Santa Lucia by its grandiose red erection
in the moonlight. Italy, she thought, Sardinia especially, is the country of towers built at the sea's edge,
towers called Saracen by a strange confusion with
the danger it was their mission to combat; as if the
ancient inhabitants of these coasts had been more
or less aware of such danger's attractions, moved by

something else than fear at the idea they might be seized and ravished and dragged aboard by one of those privateersmen that infested the Mediterranean until the beginning of the last century. To become a de luxe article, to be bathed, perfumed, polished, sold in the slave-markets of the East—sometimes the women and girls of Siniscola must have weighed such a destiny against their life of laborious misery; and had they been free to choose, where would their preference have fallen? Perhaps one girl might have run off, escaped into the dunes where Vanina was going now, when the order had been given to take refuge in the towers and to remain horribly crowded behind the thick walls until the corsairs had re-embarked.

Moreover, these men of Barbary, appearing out of the sea and the darkness, borne onward by the wind at dawn, were they not like forces of nature become men, incarnated under their turbans, armed with scimitars, shouting, laughing, grimacing like drunken apes or the goat-footed demigods common to these ancient countries?

Even while she dreamed, Vanina had made considerable progress. Walking barefoot was easier here than if she had kept her shoes. The dunes on her left, gradually diminishing, had melted into a coarse, shell-strewn beach and appeared again only when she had passed the fisheries. The girl crossed the beach—she wanted to follow the other shore, along the sound, where she knew her feet would sink up to the ankles in thick mud, unless she merely wanted to wander aimlessly a little and possibly arrive too late for the rendezvous. On the other side of the sound, under the dark trees that might be oaks, a herd of cattle was sleeping, grouped around a larger creature with tremendous horns that was perhaps a bull. Yes, that must be the bull Angela had warned them to watch out for if they went near the marsh where the children fished for crabs. During the day, when the flies annoyed him, he was dangerous, the villagers said; at night, certainly, it would be best not to disturb him.

The water was very black, and in it the reflected moon looked as if it were a comet's tail, with bloody stripes, like those on the hood of a poisonous mushroom; the marsh smelled even worse than during the day. All considerations of the bull (if it was a bull) aside, there was little to attract her in crossing the sound. The reeds that in sunlight had looked brown or yellow with green sprouts seemed gray now; bats intersected the air at various heights over the marsh, gobbling gnats, while fish leaped in rivalry for the

same prey, falling back into their element beneath
a rain of drops, and the frogs posted along the shore
frantically swelled to hurl their raucous, furious
cries to the moon, forming a kind of sonorous chain,
shortened by the sound of their dives, as Vanina
advanced upon them.

Repeated on two notes with infinitesimal vari-
ations, in a pitch that, however familiar it became,
was still astonishingly low, these croakings swelled
the night still further, as if they were made by
bronze blades set in little pairs from one end of the
island to the other and struck with tiny hammers
in indefatigable cadence. They filled Vanina's head
until it ached, keeping her from noticing how much
her feet hurt, for the tide-pool mud was more treach-
erous than the sand, concealing, aside from the
shells the sea had brought, driftwood roots with
knotty arms, coals, fish skeletons, and various sharp-
pointed debris that were not kind to the skin. "The
frog songs are grave," the girl said to herself. "It is
the voice of the earth and the water closely harmon-
ized on spring and summer nights; it is the voice of
nature, amorous and severe." She had heard this
voice rising from stagnant pools in the cities of
northern Italy, fortified with ramparts and brick
towers like opera settings, but it had taken the wild

solitude of Sardinia and the nearness of the silent
sea for the song to have the fierce authority it now
imposed.

As a result of the word "grave," the face of the
young man she was going to meet (she forgot it,
remembered it, forgot it again) returned to her memory. Then, happy to have recovered it, making an
effort not to lose it again, she held it before her eyes
with a tenderness quite new to her heart; it was a
sign, she decided, that she was a woman already,
and rejoiced. She decided that doubtless by his very
gravity the young man—lover she had instinctively
chosen the moment she saw him—was a part of this
great living nature, as much as the trees or the reeds
that seemed to move a little in the quiet air. She
thought, listening to the raucous hammering from
the throats of so many frogs, that were it not for
her love she would have felt sad, even distressed, at
the sound of their song, confronted by the trembling
of stem and leaf, in the presence of a certain tension
in earth and water alike beneath the moon's attrac-
tion which she believed she too could discern, and
which was not the least of reasons for her ecstatic
communion with the nocturnal world.

As she continued walking, the mud grew firm,
giving way to sand once more. She was at the edge

of the little channel where the water was almost
motionless; a dead fish, a feather, floated very slowly
toward the sound, for the tide had almost reached
its flow, and she passed again in front of the compli-
cated structure of stakes and boards that she and
Juliette had seen the day before, a trap (according
to Vanina's definition) and an essential instrument
of the fisheries. The ruined aspect of this edifice,
which in daylight was merely curious-looking, assumed as the moon dropped down the sky a malevo-
lent character that some viewers might have found
frightening and which derived from the proportions
distorted by the play of shadows and reflections,
from the improbable blackness of the water against
the pale phosphorescent wood, from the stakes like
poles of ruined banners, pointing ominously toward
the stars, from the shapes of some scaffold, pillory,
or catafalque. . . . Had she been willing to use the
structure as a bridge, the girl might have crossed
the channel without wetting her feet (and probably
looked down from above on the eddying, pearly
mass of captive fish within it), yet she decided not
to (despite her curiosity), and even turned away
in order to avoid approaching the first planks too
closely, and walked toward the sea.

The sea was twenty-five steps away, thirty at the

most for a narrow skirt or short legs, from which
hindrance or defect Vanina was quite free. Despite
the immobility of the air, which was no less breath-
less or oppressive than it had been during the first
half of the night (the dark cape of midnight had
been rounded over half an hour before), a slight
agitation rose within her as she neared the shore,
caused perhaps by the sea's proximity and the little
waves that regularly lapped at the sand, as if they
had rushed out from under the water after a long
journey over weedy depths since their birth in the
open sea. They reached the mouth of the canal,
subsiding until they were no longer perceptible
before they touched the stakes. She began to hear
that shallow breathing which is the sound of waves
in calm weather.

Vanina put her feet in the sea and washed them
once again, making sure they were clean of all the
filth the marsh had covered them with. She looked
at them with a gentle pity that took her by surprise
—she would gladly have polished them had her love
and her duty left her the leisure for it (and if the
beach had provided her with pumice stones); her
heart was beating a little faster, and she felt her
throat tighten. Yet she knew perfectly well that not
for all the treasures of the world (or for what would

have interested her more: the greatest surprise)
would she have turned back to security, the non-
aggression zone that had been agreed upon as if by
armistice, and she stepped farther out into the water
without bothering to lift her skirt, crossed the mouth
of the channel, wetting herself above the knees,
wetting her hands on purpose and touching herself
with them in order to be wetter still. Crabs scuttled
away from her like frightened spiders, while she
climbed up the sand on the channel's farther bank.

Her eyes again swept down the long beach that
ended at the Caletta light, as pale in the moonlight
as the reflection of the moon itself that extended,
like the paths of those divine beings who are said
to "walk upon the waves," to where it looked as if
its source would soon plummet into the sea. Here
was where the Region Perilous began (if the handsome plunderer had interpreted the assignation
properly), and it was deserted, as far as the eye
could reach. The reeds bordering the inland marsh
grew within a few yards of the gulf shore, which
here was rather steep, gullied by rain, strewn with
detritus of all sizes—a tree with all its branches
and roots, broken boxes, old planks, pieces of wood,
a scattering of tiny corks—and was passable only by
means of a difficult path over the rocks or another,

below, across the spongy sand and the shifting water.

Vanina decided on the lower path, since she was too wet not to resign herself to being more so. Her skirt, which usually reached below her knees, now hung to her ankles; the sodden silk stretched as though weighted with lead and stuck to her skin like the cotton shifts the village girls wore bathing, irremediably spoiled by the salt water; the damage evident to eye and touch alike, so much costly material ruined, introduced a principle of destruction that forecast the abandon of her body and that developed within her to the accompaniment of a new, superb intoxication. Aside from this sacrificial rapture, there was still room in her mind for a certain apprehension. The reeds on the slope of the sandy ridge clashed together without apparent cause, for the air was as calm as ever, and they made a noise of canes against each other, to which the girl listened mistrustfully. She looked at the clumps of tall, silver-gray rushes and wondered if the ravisher she expected, or someone else, was hidden within them, if someone would come toward her out of the reeds, would lay hands upon her and fling her to the ground. She looked behind her to be sure no one was following her, for with this new idea that it was not impossible to fall prey to a stranger, someone quite different from the chosen lover, her fear of the carabiniers rose again, since she knew they often made their rounds with dogs during the night, looking for smugglers here on the beach. How could she escape those terrible dogs, how shield herself from the gallantry of their masters, troublesome enough in daylight and in public? Rather than let herself be taken by one of these men, whom she detested for their uniform, their military odor, and their vulgar accent, she would have prayed for a beard to sprout on her face, like that Iberian virgin miraculously preserved from the pagans about to ravish her, and whose face the ancient pilgrims believed they could recognize on the image of the Sindon. Her sense of humor persisting beneath her fear, she told herself that a carabinier could in no way be considered an incarnation of great Panic nature!

Beyond a little spit protruding into the gulf, probably the alluvial deposit of the canal, the terrain changed, or rather recovered its earlier aspect. The reeds retreated to the inland shore, curving along the brackish water and leaving a row of pines behind them in the central plain. The beach was as wide, the sand as even and fine as toward Santa Lucia di Siniscola. Between the pines and the sea, rose more dunes, higher and broader, it seemed, than those near the village or the fisheries. Above all, the solitude was more complete, for once past the two obstacles of the canal and the constricted zone, Vanina sensed that all contact had been broken with the houses of Santa Lucia, and those of La Caletta were too far away, the lighthouse hidden behind the trees, to give the impression of a human presence, an inhabited region. There was no sound of life save the song of the frogs in the distance, repeated so often that she ceased to hear it save when she made a point of listening for it. The carabiniers, except on special patrols, never pushed their explorations into this desert.

Then it was, while she was walking on with less assured steps (for she was tired, having come so far), and wondering if she should go any farther, or sit on the sand to dream until daybreak, or even return to the cottage, she saw him appear between two low dunes crowned with euphorbias and lilies. The moon, almost on a level with the waves behind her, lit up his face as if he were on a stage. He was very handsome, yes, her first impressions had not deceived her, and the reality of his face, bright against the surrounding darkness, reduced to inept sketches everything the young girl had struggled to

recapture by memory, wrestling with the wear that
leaves no recalled object perfectly intact. Here then
was the man who was to be "the lover," the one she
loved and had come to find in the lonely darkness.
She felt herself stumble, no longer from fatigue, and
her weakness was all the worse, or better, when she
saw that though he was not wearing a jacket, nevertheless a long red tie (a knitted one that did not
widen at the ends) hung down over his shirt, while
his sleeves were rolled far up his arms.

That she had not heard him approach, as on that
other afternoon, in the pine woods, was not at all
extraordinary, for he was evidently waiting for her,
motionlessly spying on her for several minutes, hidden in a hollow of the sand, and then suddenly he
had stood up, like a huge puppet in black breeches,
when he had seen her within reach on the sand.
"Puppet?" The word, even if suggested by this the-
atrical light in which the young man had risen up
before her, was scarcely one to be applied without
derision to a lover's person. Vanina had no time to
reflect on this detail, for this same person had left
the ideal scene in which she contemplated him. He
had reached her in several long strides of his espadrilles, and he had seized her.

It was only by the arm, but even that was enough

for her to know she was a captive, so long had she imagined this gesture and estimated the weight of this hand laid upon her. "Everything is beginning," she thought, and thought too that love was a duplicity if not a contradiction, since its beginning, materially too, was a weight added no less than a stripping away. She had one anxiety left, which related to a certain desire she had expressed to him at their first meeting and which she feared he no longer remembered. "Don't talk," she said. "Keep still."

He smiled almost gently. The rule of silence would not embarrass him.

Sliding his hand down her arm without releasing her, he made the girl turn before him, seized the other wrist from behind, and drew both arms out straight. She could feel his breath on the nape of her neck and hear the panting sound it made, like an animal scenting its prey. Then he made her turn around entirely, as in a dance, and let her go, but his eyes weighed upon her without permitting her the slightest liberty. He slowly untied his necktie and drew it off; Vanina admired him for acting so calmly.

She was proud to love, and she was proud too of having chosen her lover so well; she was proud of having come barefoot to him, barefoot since the be-

ginning of the beach; she was proud to feel that he
was binding her hands behind her back now as she
had told him to do not long ago, and she was proud
of having had the initiative to give this command,
to have conceived this binding which he would
never have thought of himself, for certainly it took
a woman, even a virgin, to realize that this position
—arms wrenched behind the back, wrists bound
together—was the indispensable complement of bare
feet.

When he was finished with his task, which he
performed with no gratuitous harshness, but thoroughly, drawing the knots tight, he stepped back
two or three steps to examine his conquest. Vanina
remained impassive and yielded herself to his gaze
as if already to his hands. There was no need to be
a sybil to realize the young man's astonishment that
she had submitted to the first test with no appearance of rebellion, and that she had come to him,
yielded herself to his will, surrendered herself as his
captive, offered herself to his bonds, just as she had
promised, but as he had not dared to hope she would
in truth. It must have been a great wonder for him
to discover she had not been joking at all (as certain
women had, perhaps) in the pine grove, and that
she would keep her promise to the last extremity;

but did he suspect to what degree the wonder was all the greater for her, thus to abandon herself to love, and to will to be free no longer, out of the pure fanaticism of her amorous cause? Besides, could he have even a notion of such love?

Now he came close to her again, and seized her once more. With one hand, after he released the shoulder, he took possession of the armpit offered by the sleeveless blouse; the other gently pulled the lower part of her blouse out of her skirt, so that her waist was laid bare. His fingers had undone the first button of her collar, and the second, and the girl watched him bending down to savor the smell of her again, and she rejoiced at this action of which he probably did not know the meaning—that according to the rules of ancient Oriental magic, there was a formidable power conferred on the captor who knew the odors of a captive body. She realized that all the time he was caressing her waist beneath the blouse, he was pushing her forward, and she obediently began walking in the indicated direction, making no gesture that he had not imposed, not permitting herself, as she suddenly desired, to lean her cheek against his.

They passed between the two dunes where he had first appeared and descended into a hollow

which offered concealment enough, but which was
not where he had decided to take her, for he continued to impel her onward, and she had to climb
the opposite slope (which was not easy for her,
bound as she was); the sand, under its thin crust,
crumbled beneath her at every step. There was a
still higher dune to climb, then they walked along
its summit. Spiny thistles, so small she could scarcely
discern them against the sand of the same color,
pricked her feet several times, and then she had the
impression of being more completely subjugated,
more closely bound by the pain of these scratches.

After climbing down the other side of this dune,
they followed a path that soon led into a rounded
valley, enclosed on all sides by the dunes. The sand
was smooth here, and finer than on the beach itself,
with no thistles, weeds, or briars, free of insects and
shells, clear of dead things and debris, showing no
footprint or track, perfectly virgin. The dunes around
it bore a profuse growth of sea lilies, whose perfume
seemed concentrated in this hollow. What word
could apply better than "arena" to this place, which
was circular in shape, or actually slightly oval? In
this arena, then, where the young man had brought
his captive, the shadow of the dunes left a large
central area of moonlight. It was this area that he

pointed to, careful to say nothing, according to their tacit law, and then he pressed upon her and forced her to lie down upon the sand.

Swift fingers rushed to open her blouse, despite the stiffening of the wet buttonholes, were quick to slide everywhere under her skirt, skilful, never still, brushing so lightly over her hips, her round calves, her long thighs, and her ankles, that she did not know when or how the thin envelope of red nylon had disappeared. She was feeling, then, all she had desired—all she had asked to be made to feel. In her satisfaction, it occurred to her that their pleasure held within it something too much of exactitude, followed too faithfully the program established in advance. The girl wanted to determine for herself that her lover had the qualities of a real aggressor, that he was stronger than she, as he must be to be worthy of her love; or else he was merely obeying her instructions of the day before, and in that case he would have deceived her, and she would have withdrawn from his embrace.

"No," she said, clenching her teeth, contracting her limbs like a crab taken out of water. "Don't touch me. Untie me. Let me go."

He merely smiled at her words, as if to show he had understood her perfectly, but his eyes grew so

fierce, his expression so stern, that she soon saw the
absurdity of pleading, of promising, or commanding,
since obviously nothing short of murder would keep
him from working his will upon her.

Then Vanina abandoned herself body and soul to
the pain and the pleasure of knowing herself a help-
less creature, conquered, seized, bound, thrown to
the ground, handled without indulgence, her every
intimacy rifled, every secret exposed, and she realized she was "in love's power" (as the expression
has it), and she imagined the soft muzzles of the
cows, the majestic trees all leaning over her together
at the consummation of this inhuman and splendid
sacrifice. The moonlight flooded the sand, its whiteness blinding at the level of the girl's eyes. The sea
lilies had another whiteness, aureoled with fire, on
their pointed foliage that also gleamed in the moonlight over the tops of the dunes, and their perfume
rolled to the floor of the arena in a wave heavier and
more powerful than ever. Vanina's breasts were offered to the moon, magnificently high and naked
(for the plunderer had not been slow to open the
clasps behind her back and throw away the useless
brassiere); she saw them swollen as if they had fed
on the nectar of the lilies, or floated in their fragrance as on a heavy liquid, and she delighted in the

unexpected revelation, not of a resemblance, but of a kind of essential analogy, a relation between her breasts and these waxen flowers and the moon itself.

An owl, which could not have been a large one, had flown over them several times, almost at the height of the dunes, hunting bats that fled by sudden dives and zigzags in the air. The light grew dimmer with every moment.

Vanina remembered (she would not have been able to say from what depths the recollection sprang) a fragment of one of Mérimée's letters about a pretty girl encountered in Madrid. This young creature, when she had been asked: "Did that hurt you," had savagely replied, "When you love a man, he could have a red-hot piece of iron there, and you would not feel the pain of it!" Then Vanina thought that she was wrong always to be mingling these souvenirs of culture with the business of life itself, and that it would be good to try to become, like Juliette, an animal.

But she did not cry out when she felt the burning of the iron.

After having yielded to her lover completely, and after he had withdrawn from her, Vanina looked at him. The moon had disappeared below the horizon now, for the lilies that had been incandescent beneath its last beams just a moment before had gone out like lamps, but the stars shone with increased splendor, and provided enough light to see by still. He untied her; this rag that had been a blouse, pushed back to her wrists, rolled into a ball, crushed beneath her loins, twisted by the movements of their struggle, soiled with wet salt, fell away. Happy to feel herself completely naked on the sand, she gave herself to him with a skill that derived in part from her reading, in part from what she had just learned in practice, and more from the handsome grave body she had carefully examined before pressing herself against it once more. "A man must be strong, but above all he must be grave," she thought.

He remained within her for a long time. The soft noise of the waves, forty yards away, indulged their union like the hand of a benevolent god, and the meteors (it was the season when they are common on cloudless nights) occasionally streaked the sky with their orange fire.

Later, he took her again.

Vanina's hair had worked into the sand like roots, a mouth, fishlike, grazed her thighs, her naked belly, a hard knee knocked against her forehead. "There is nothing so marvelous as love," she thought, as the

limits of her selfhood dropped away, naïvely over-
whelmed, intoxicated with pleasure, filled with a
presence so enormous and superhuman that at last
she felt, as she had so desired to feel, "in communi-
cation with all of nature."

An infinite goodness forced her beyond herself.
She needed to speak, to hear, to groan. She would
have liked to console . . .

"I know you, now," she said. "You have to love
someone to know him."

Then, the words bringing sentences to her mind,
developing them into memories, the memories opening out into flowering images like corals in a cloudy
pool: "I am yours," she said, "by right of jetsam—
the way everything abandoned on the shore belongs
to the owner of the land. You are the owner of the
land, my darling, fabulous, grave lover. I am a petty
thing, the sweepings of the sea, a piece of wreckage,
seaweed, yes, a floating weed, a clot of foam; a poor
blood-stained thing washed up on the sand under
the stars. It is not from tonight, I want you to know
that, not from tonight that I am blood-stained, nor
from yesterday, nor even the day before. I shall tell
you a story I do not often tell, I want you to understand. My father and my mother were murdered. I
would have been killed with them if I had been

there, as I should have been, and if they had not sent me to my nurse's house in Switzerland to be safe from the bombings. Yes, I would have been murdered too, certainly, and sometimes, at night, I am almost ashamed not to have been, but now I'm glad, because this way I have had the happiness to meet you, to come to you barefoot, and to feel inside myself the rip, the rending, the explosion of your strength, your calm strength. Yes, my father and my mother were both murdered. I have the sign of blood, as you say in this country. It was at the end of the war, in their villa near Bergamo, on a night as warm as this, probably: some patriots (or so they were called) forced open the door. They were described to me as young men wearing dark clothes, with red scarves around their necks and long hair down to their shoulders, either because that was the fashion or to signify the wild life they were living in the mountains. Some were handsome, or so they say. First they killed the old servant who had led them into the hall where the statues were, and then they took my parents out to the little garden, to a place where I used to play lady when I was a little girl—there was a pink stone fountain with benches and more statues and tall black cypresses pointing straight up into the pale sky. They questioned my

parents, because they wanted money, and my mother
gave them all the jewels she had on, even her wedding ring, but that wasn't enough, probably (the
most valuable ones were in the bank), because they
tied her up and raped her on the edge of the fountain, in front of my father whom they had tied to
the statue of Hercules. I remember my mother very
well. She wasn't old, and I think I'm supposed to
look like her. You might have loved her, if you were
older. Then the patriots killed them both, one after
the other, with a bullet in the neck, and the water
in the fountain ran red with blood. They confessed
to everything when they were arrested a few years
later, and were tried in court. I think they were
beaten to make them speak, according to the custom,
but they weren't killed, I wonder why. When I
think about it, I prefer knowing they were left alive.
Perhaps one of them looked like you. . . . You can
kill me if you like, since you have already bound me
and raped me, and I have this blood on me, but I
think you will not kill me, since you have untied me,
and you are looking at me with pity in your eyes."

He kissed her breasts. "Will he love me?" she
wondered, for she had few illusions about the capac-
ity of young men to love. Then she thought again,
"That he is handsome and grave, and that I love him

—that is what is important. It is not absolutely necessary that he love me; it is not even indispensable that he have a soul, that he be inhabited by a kind of sea gull."

The silence had fallen again, since she had no further desire to speak and he continued to say nothing; they played with each other's bodies a while longer, but like curious children rather than with the passion and the violence their pleasures had required at first. Exploring, they admired each other. At last she sent him away, when he insisted on accompanying her to the fisherman's cottage.

"No," she said. "Leave me. Perhaps I would be ashamed to wash myself in front of you; and I need to be alone to think about myself, to find out how much I love you."

A little blood had dried on her thighs, like a precious piece of black lace. Naked still, holding in her hand the clothes she had picked up after his departure, she walked to the beach where she put them down, and went into the sea. The water was not cold. A few birds were flying low in the sky, their cries heralding the day; the night began to grow transparent.

She swam out to sea, letting her hair stream behind her, and she saw how alone she was on the dark, stirring surface, and she knew she would come to the end of her strength sooner than usual. She was tempted to die, but she was afraid of the souls, for the gulls screamed not far over her head; besides, the word "suicide" had always seemed so ugly to her, signifying an act that revolted her nature, like the words "evasion" or "betrayal." She was not sorry when her feet felt the sand beneath them once again.

Then came the first fit of chills. Vanina wrung out her hair, dried herself as well as she could, rubbing her body with the tiny red panties, cursing the nylon that could not absorb water. Then she threw them to the waves, which swelled them up and carried them off like a great flower or a purple jellyfish. It was not easy to dress herself decently with what was left of her clothes, but their ruined appearance—buttons torn from the blouse, the skirt ripped, the crumpled silk clinging to her wet skin—filled the girl with joy and pride. "Who could deny," she told herself, "that love has been upon me? Why did I put my brassiere back on? I should have come home waving it over my head, like a flag. I wish the whole world could see me!"

Perhaps she did, but for notable witnesses there were only the gulls and cormorants, not worth brandishing her banner, or sounding her trumpets; Va-

nina had to resign herself to making her way home
in solitude. It was a slower trip than it had been in
the opposite direction, although by a shorter route,
for she was racked with aches, and in her womb
grew a subtle pain that kept her from walking at
her usual pace. But from this fact of pain itself she
drew a certain satisfaction, for she took it as proof
she was not the dupe of a dream (so many times she
had dreamed of blood, and of walking alone at daybreak along interminable beaches). She might have
dreamed the pain, too, in the worst cases, but such
an eventuality was scarcely acceptable now, because
of this sense of a sovereign presence she had already
known and which the pain revived so strongly. It
was as if a little of her lover had detached itself, like
the hornet's sting left in the wound, so that she bore
it within herself, like a relic. And she wondered if
he was suffering from the loss of what was now in
her cherished keeping.

She crossed the canal; the current there was violent when the ebb-tide drained the sound into the
sea. Farther on she saw the tower of Santa Lucia
dark against the paling sky. It was almost daylight
when she reached the stump that marked the spot
where her slippers were; she found them where she
had left them, under the crocodile (which had noth-

ing of its moonlight wickedness now). Putting them on, she walked even more slowly, but more firmly, toward the town.

The boats had put out to sea in her absence, before dawn, as usual, and there were only a few dinghies left on the beach. A woman who was standing on her long skirt among the anchors wrapped her black veil around her when she saw the stranger coming down the beach, staring without a greeting or any word at all, her expression one of refusal rather than scorn or surprise. Wryly Vanina told herself she was returning to the world of work, leaving the world of love.

Having met no one except this emblem of severity, she returned to her room as she had left it. The house was perfectly still.

Did she sleep? No; she remembered. Then she took off her "lover's habit" and rolled it into a ball in the corner of her suitcase. Less oddly dressed, she went in and wakened Juliette, forced her to get up, dress, make tea, pack her bags. They were leaving, yes they were, right now, before the heat grew stifling; there were lots of other things to see in Sardinia besides the beach at Santa Lucia di Siniscola, where they had stayed too long already. As a great concession, if she insisted, Juliette had permission to be photographed once again in front of the Saracen tower.

When she heard the news, Angela's lamentations were loud and long; had something displeased her lodgers (perhaps the little girl cried too much, or was it the black beetles, greedy for sugar and artificial silk), would they at least put off their departure until noon, so Francesco could say goodbye, give them a live lobster out of the day's catch. Juliette, easily moved, was soon on Signora Carone's side, but Vanina was inflexible. She paid (generously, for consolation was obligatory), dragged the luggage to the doorstep, loaded the mousekin. The starter did its work. It was not eight o'clock before they were on their way out of the village, on a stony lane between the pines and eucalyptus trees.

Since Vanina said nothing, once they were in the car and on their way, Juliette, after grumbling a while, fell asleep. Vanina drove with a scrupulous care that owed everything to habit and nothing to her present state of mind. The latter, in fact, was detached, and exultant. To such a degree that the girl attained a state that was a kind of pure rapture, and stopped the car for a moment to yield herself to it more completely. They were on the road to Orosei, in the midst of a deep valley ("the Andes," she thought) where the surrounding mountains hid the sea, though she could still hear it, and where the scrubby meadows spread for several miles on every side. With a terrible greed, as if this might have been her last look, Vanina stared at the gray peaks tearing the violent blue of the sky, the rust and purple distances, the great scattered blocks speckled with lichen, the savagely striped and spotted rocks. She contemplated a dry stream bed and the veins of pebbles, the stony outcrops at the foot of the mountains, the dust on the ground, the thorny trees and bushes, the wiry grass; she followed the flight of birds, the leaps of insects, she listened to their various cries and calls, their buzzes and hums, and she felt herself overflowing with an immense tenderness in which everything she saw and heard participated, a tenderness like a whirlwind inside her, and for its center, if not its motive, deep within herself, was the sustained presence of her lover.

"I'm glad," she said to herself, "I wasn't foolish enough to ask him his name. Love has no use for labels."

And she started up the car again.